GOD DOES NOT EAT MEAT

ARTHUR POLETTI

The author obtained Copyright Certificate of Registration

March 23, 2004.

Arthur Poletti © Copyright 2004 and 2006

British Library Cataloguing In Publication Data
A Record of this Publication is available
from the British Library

ISBN 1846852315
978-1-84685-231-2

Published 2006 by

Exposure Publishing, an imprint of Diggory Press,
Three Rivers, Minions, Liskeard, Cornwall, PL14 5LE, UK
WWW.DIGGORYPRESS.COM

PRINTED IN THE USA ON ACID FREE PAPER

Everybody exists. It is only the few who live.
To live, you should have an IDEAL.

Life is short. The path is long. The pinnacle
is very high. The time is very little.

Swami Chinmayananda

Acknowledgments

Thank you to Pamela Rice, founder of the
Vegetarian Center of NYC for permission
to use (parts of) 22 reasons from her
101 Reasons Why I'm A Vegetarian.

Pamela can be contacted at:
Pamela Rice
P.O. Box 294
Prince Street Station New York, NY 10012-0005
E-mail pamela@vivavegie.org

Thanks to Hinduism Today,
http://hinduismtoday.com, for allowing me
to use parts of "How To Win An Argument
With A Meat Eater."

For information contact:
Sannyasin Arumugaswami
Managing Editor
Hinduism Today
107 Kaholalele Road
Kapaa, Hawaii 96746 USA
Phone 808-822-7032, ext.227
Fax 808-822-4351

Thanks to Chinmaya Publications,
www.chinmayapublications.org for allowing me to use parts of
The Journey Called Life:
The Light of Wisdom: and
The Vision of Life
For information contact:
Swami Siddhananda
560 Bridgetowne Pike
Langhorne, Pa 19053
Phone: 215-396-0390
Fax: 215-396-9710

Thanks to Neal D. Barnard, M.D.
Physicians Committee for Responsible Medicine
for allowing me to use one of his famous quotations.

Dedication

I was inspired by my intuitive communications with animals, the earth, and God to write this story. Especially to honor the precious, irreplaceable, and sacred God given life of each and every vulnerable animal that has been or will be killed in a slaughterhouse. Every vulnerable animal that has or will experience the cruelty and horror of factory farm systems while being raised for slaughter. Every vulnerable animal that has been or will be hunted and killed for sport, and every vulnerable animal that has or will suffer during the gruesome process of laboratory experimentation.

While they innocently stand in line in slaughterhouses throughout the world waiting for their lives to be violently destroyed, innocent, frightened, and terrified animals desperately try to communicate with humans. If you listen carefully you can hear them now. They are saying, please let me live, please do not kill me. What did I do wrong that makes you want to kill me?

I have a hidden deep rooted sick feeling every day, that I disguise well, as I consciously and subconsciously think about the huge number of animals that live short horrendous lives before they are brutally killed, which is totally unnecessary.

Hopefully most of the people that read this story will determine there are profoundly obvious and convincing reasons why every vulnerable animal deserves the opportunity to live a full life surrounded by an atmosphere filled with safety, peace, tranquility, and kindness.

How can humans ever expect to stop killing each other if they cannot do something as simple as not eating meat and not killing animals?

I am certain that God did not put animals on earth so they could be tortured, killed, and eaten by humans.

Contents

Foreword 11

Chapter One: 17

A Life of Kindness, Dreams of Cruelty

Chapter Two: 29
How Kindness to Animals Has Changed the World

Chapter Three: 35

How Bad Things Used to Be

Chapter Four: 41
More Benefits from Protecting Animals

Chapter Five: 49
More Fertile Land, More Prosperous Farmers

Chapter Six: 55
Great Companions, Wonderful Helpers

Chapter Seven: 57
Before We Knew We Really Cared

Chapter Eight: 65
Stop Hunting - Start Protecting

Chapter Nine: 71
Choose Kindness and Life, Renounce Cruelty and Death

Chapter Ten: 87
There Are No Slaughterhouses in Heaven

Epilogue: 101

Foreword

Mahatma Gandhi once said, "The greatness of a nation and its moral progress can be measured by the way in which its animals are treated. To my mind, the life of a lamb is no less precious than that of a human being."

This story presents a case for the importance and absolute necessity of continually attempting to protect and preserve all animal life. Hopefully, the story provides reasonable and believable predictions of a multitude of positive affects that could occur as a result of REMOVING ALL MEATS FROM THE FOOD CHAIN for humans and animals in the United States, and in as many other countries as possible.

Together we will take a journey on a path rarely traveled. During our exploration we will utilize words of wisdom expressed by some of the most famous people in history to help create a story that unleashes a fierce battle between two entirely different societies. Within this format we will theoretically deploy the awesome power of non-violence to wage a war against life's most formidable insidious adversary.

Cruelty, the abetting loyal servant and evil partner of violence, is the most devastating and most difficult dilemma for human and animal life to contend with, and has proven to be one of the most difficult problems to solve or even control.

Every person should continually inspire their consciousness to inquire and seek their own personal truth about life's most important issues. Only then can one develop the feeling of real compassion that comes from understanding and wisdom. The decisions you make after reading this story could reveal some of your deepest true feelings, especially concerning the value and importance of every animal's life.

You may be inspired and motivated to support and be a part of this cause and hopefully be convinced that this seemingly impossible fairy tale could become reality.

You may also be persuaded to consider and decide, for your spiritual salvation, which society you would prefer to live in, and conversely which society you would prefer to die in.

Imagine living during the period in history when meat is removed from the food chain in the United States and all slaughterhouses are closed.

Imagine!

Think about some of the happy times you have experienced in your life, especially the laughter and joyous moments spent with your family and friends. Remember your childhood and how your parents loved, protected, and provided for you. Remember the thrill and excitement of your wedding day and the births of your children. Remember the animals you have loved and cared for that have meant so much to you.

What you probably never realized or preferred not to think about is that during every minute of your life—past, present, and future—animals have been and will be tortured, killed, and consumed by most of the human race.

Every ardent vegan and vegetarian in the world who truly cares about animal welfare must absolutely come out of the closet now and be heard. Thousands of years of cruelty to animals are enough.

Several million people need to join forces and organize a relentless campaign making as many people as possible aware of the magnitude of cruelty that exists to animals and the worldwide catastrophic disaster meat consumption has caused.

The detestable, needless, never ending mass murder of animals and consumption of their flesh must stop now.

One day soon we will rejoice when slaughterhouses begin closing because of the lack of demand for meat. One by one the horrible houses of murder will close until every slaughterhouse in the Unites States is out of business and eradicated forever.

The importance of this point of view is supported and summed up brilliantly by one of the most renowned men in history.

"For as long as men massacre animals, they will kill each other. Indeed, he who sows the seed of murder and pain cannot reap joy and love."

Pythagoras, mathematician

Authors that have been sympathetic to hunters insist that the Bible's Judeo-Christian teaching, especially the commandment Thou shall not kill, refers only to humans, not to animals. They conclude that hunting or slaughtering animals for food consumption is not condemned in the Bible and therefore cannot be sacrilegious. They argue that it has always been the hunter's God-given right to hunt and kill, making reference to passages in the Bible that in fact support their arguments.

The sacred Bible was written over 2000 years ago by men who had the special somewhat dubious self invoked talent to explicitly express Gods will. The Bible is quite accommodating because it contains no passages that clearly condemn killing animals for food. Moreover, it contains commands for animal sacrifices in the Old Testament.

Throughout history, most people who have been sympathetic to animals have also eaten meat, and hundreds of millions have hunted and killed animals. On the one hand they have loved and cared for their pets, but on the other hand most of the human race has condoned, supported, or participated in the biggest ongoing atrocity ever known. Amoral people throughout the world have the ability to look the other way and feel no guilt or remorse for the crimes they support and commit toward animals. The age-old saying out of sight, out of mind could not be more appropriate.

It is a strange and unfortunate paradox that in order to perceive and appreciate the all encompassing importance of kindness and non-violence one must become fully aware of the scope and magnitude of the never ending disaster caused by the worst kind of cruelty and violence.

Now with the benefit of ageless words of wisdom and insight, we can clearly predict how much better off the world could be if all animals were emancipated and not killed for food or sport, or tortured and killed during laboratory experimentations.

From time to time an ancient philosophy needs an intelligent reinterpretation in the context of the new times. Men of wisdom, prophets, and seers must guide the common man as to how he can apply the ancient laws effectively to his present pattern of life.

Swami Chinmayananda

Our story begins in 2065; just fifty-seven years after the United States Congress officially instituted the New Revolutionary Animal Welfare Act. The laws that were formally adopted on September 1, 2008, were designed to protect all animals from being killed for any reason other than a human's self-defense if attacked by an animal, or to end an animal's suffering from an injury. These laws forbade any type of hunting or slaughter as well as the consumption of any type of animal meat, and they outlined severe penalties for needlessly killing or committing any act of cruelty toward any animal. The laws have been strictly enforced for fifty-seven years.

Law enforcement agencies have maintained carefully monitored records of persons known to be cruel to animals. Records have been scrutinized and are considered to be as important as the laws that are enforced to protect people. All persons who own animals or are planning to purchase an animal must carry a coded certified card that verifies that the card carrier has a record of never committing any act of cruelty to any animal.

It is against the law for people with proven records of cruelty to animals to harbor, care for, or own pets. Additionally, it is against the law for any business to sell a pet to any person or business with a record for being cruel to any animal.

The names of all persons who have been prosecuted for acts of cruelty to animals are made available to businesses and the general public over the internet or can be obtained at law enforcement agencies.

Persons buying an animal for the first time must sign a contract acknowledging that they have read and understand the penalties for cruelty to animals. Substantial rewards are paid to any person who informs the police about people they have witnessed being cruel to an animal. The rewards are immediately paid upon verification and proof of the allegation.

Violations to stray or homeless animals will also result in large fines and or imprisonment for needlessly killing or committing any act of cruelty to any animal. The proof of any

15

domestic act of cruelty to any animal results in the same punishment with the likely removal of the animal or animals from the offender's home.

During each of the first five years that these laws were in effect in the United States, thousands of people were fined and hundreds went to prison. In 2064, two hundred and forty seven people were fined and five were sent to prison.

Webster's dictionary defines a barbarian as a wild, cruel, uncivilized person. The United States Animal Welfare Act of 2008 is often referred to as the beginning of the end of the age of the barbarian—an age that began with prehistoric man.

Chapter One

A Life of Kindness, Dreams of Cruelty

Bradford Knox was about to begin the final stages of his last semester as a student at the University of California. One of the last requirements needed to graduate with the class of 2065 was to produce a philosophy thesis proving that the world is better off today because of reforms made as a result of human wisdom. The thesis would be presented to his classmates over several days of one-hour speeches. The assignment seemed like a gift from heaven. Bradford had enormous compassion for animals and was well educated regarding the current conditions of animal welfare. He decided he would provide a comprehensive presentation that would explain how much better off the United States and much of the world is today simply because of kindness to animals.

Over the weekend Brad discussed his plans with his girlfriend Alyssa. Many of her relatives had been vegetarians long before 2008. Besides being absolutely gorgeous, Alyssa also has a brilliant mind, a wonderful personality, a beautiful smile, and is the kindest and most unselfish person Brad has ever known. After two days of discussions with Brad she wanted to offer her advise and recommendations for what she thought would be the most effective and convincing method to deliver his speech. Alyssa grabbed Bradford's hand to get his attention, and then began to voice her opinions.

"Bradford, I think you should devote the first part of your report explaining how animals have been treated in the United States since meat was taken out of the food chain in 2008. Specifically, you should highlight how nearly 57 years of kindness to animals (from 2008 to 2065) has immensely improved our society.

"Then in order to make impressive and compelling comparisons I think you should gather extensive information regarding the conditions that existed for animals in the United States prior to 2008.

17

"In my opinion, along with your self-knowledge you will gain more clarity, meaningful understanding, and a clearer vision of the overall subject through more of your own observations and inquiries.

"For these reasons I also suggest that you refer to books written by members of some of the many animal rights groups that waged a long worldwide battle to improve the lives of animals prior to 2008.

"So what do you think?" said Alyssa.

Brad smiled and said, "Alyssa, you are absolutely correct. In addition to reading, I will observe and evaluate films depicting animal cruelty so that I can develop a more accurate perspective as to how horrible the conditions were once like."

Brad and Alyssa had dinner and discussed the subject for the remainder of the evening.

Each night Brad begrudgingly viewed outrageous and gut wrenching films that vividly and explicitly depicted the grotesque massacre of large numbers of precious animals. He also read factual accounts of the cruelty and mass murder of animals that existed for thousands of years until 2008. Most evenings would end with Brad dozing off into a fantasy dream world of horror. The dreams, which were sporadic at first, always seemed to start the same way, with a more real-than-life account of the killings that had occurred. He would find himself in a pastoral setting driving down a country road on a bright glorious day admiring the sun, the clouds, and the earth. Then the picture would change to frightening mind flashes of a variety of different animals being tortured and killed in slaughterhouses.

The people in his dream seemed to enjoy killing animals in a brutal and heartless way with no concern for the pain, agony, and suffering each animal experienced. Brad's nightmares were far too real and began to tear him apart emotionally. He would grimace and quiver imagining the suffering, excruciating pain, and death that millions of animals once experienced every day in the United States.

During his conscious hours in the present, Brad tried to think of ways he could stop the carnage he saw in his dreams. The disgusting dreams of unimaginable cruelty and killing began to change his current life to one of sadness and grief. He became so outraged; he began to think the only answer was to kill the killers. While Brad pondered the use of violence as an option, he remembered a Hindu saying that one of his childhood teachers, Professor Monrovia, used to repeat to him often written by Swami Sivananda.

To be free from violence is the duty of every man. No thought of revenge, hatred or ill will should arise in our minds. Injuring others gives rise to hatred.

Brad, normally robust, outspoken, and happy, became introverted, quiet, and lethargic. He had difficulty speaking to his classmates and often began to sweat and squirm in class. His classmates and friends were shaken and concerned by his behavior.

Then some dreams took him to the many horrors of deer hunting season and in his dreams he tried to find some way to stop the hunters. Because Brad's natural instincts are to protect, and care for animals, he approached the hunters and pleaded to them not to kill the deer. One of the hunters laughed at Brad and told him hunting was a sport for real men, not sissies, and then told Brad go home to his mother.

In the next dream Brad saw two laughing hunters returning from a kill with a dead deer. Brad thought of another method that might work to stop the killing, so he followed the hunters as they placed the deer into a storage area then walked into a tavern. He decided to approach them at the bar. Brad realized the time period he was in when he noticed one of the hunters reading a sports section of the Chicago Tribune dated Saturday, March 15, 1986. He exchanged introductions with several people at the bar, saying he just moved into town. He began a conversation with a hunter named Mondo Pacenti who had already dragged several dead deer from the woods.

"How did the hunt go?" Brad asked.

"I bagged five deer."

"What will you do with them?"

"I'll keep one head to mount over my fireplace," said Mondo, "and I have customers who will purchase the remaining heads. The butchered venison will be cut into portions that I will give to friends who love the taste.

"Where did you learn how to be so adept with a rifle?"

"I'm a Vietnam veteran; and I did a tour of duty in the Special Forces where I became a marksman."

"Just out of curiosity, there are many objects that could be used as targets to shoot at that are not live animals. Why do you need or choose to kill animals?"

"Don't tell me you are one of those animal rights weirdo's!" exclaimed Mondo.

"Yes, as a matter of fact I am," answered Brad.

"I bet you don't eat meat, either."

"That is correct."

"I know your type," said Mondo. "You wear leather shoes and belts and your car has leather seats, and you think that's okay, right?"

"Wrong. I wear canvas shoes and belts made from cloth, and my car seats are covered with fabric."

"Are you one of those veggie people?

"I am a vegan."

"What's that?"

"A simple explanation is that animals do not have to be tortured and killed so that I can eat. The meals I eat come from nature's menu of earth-grown foods that provide a large variety of much healthier choices."

"Everyone I know eats meat," objected Mondo, "and I have always eaten meat. So have my parents and my grandparents. I cannot imagine not eating meat."

"Everyone I know does not eat meat," said Brad, "and I have never eaten meat. I cannot imagine eating meat. Have dinner with me sometime and we will have a vegan meal. There are many choices available that taste great and are much healthier for you. The best part is that animals do not have to die. Why not give it a try?"

"Okay, I am willing to do that, just as long as you don't mind if I throw up all over you when I am done."

"That sounds fair." replied Brad.

"Where do you live?" asked Mondo.

"Laguna Niguel, California."

"What are you doing here?"

"I have been dreaming, and you are in my dream."

"Are you one of those sick wacko types trying to convince people you can time travel?"

"No, I am perfectly sane, but I am from a different time and a different town."

"I think you are a nut case from la-la land and need to talk to a shrink as soon as possible.

"I suppose you can come here from a different time and place whenever you like, right?"

"I am not sure about that," said Brad, "but somehow I think a greater power is responsible for creating this meeting, and I have no idea for what reason."

Mondo obviously did not believe any of Brad's stories about being from another time and place, but he could not help enjoying Brad's seemingly clairvoyant imagination and his techniques for trying to persuade Mondo to stop hunting animals and eating meat. Just then Brad woke up from his dream and was amazed at how real it all seemed. He could only hope to somehow return to the same time and place again to continue conversing with Mondo.

The last and most important step for Brad to take before his school presentation was to visit with an Indian psychologist and philanthropist, Professor Deepak Monrovia, to discuss two important topics. First, he wanted to seek his advice about the meaning of his nightmares, especially his dream that included the deer hunter Mondo Pacenti. Second, he wanted to get recommendations for his upcoming classroom presentation.

Professor Monrovia is a handsome, healthy, ninety-seven-year-old Indian yogi prophet who retired in 2030 after teaching for thirty-two years at the University of California. He had been a teacher and advisor to Brad since Brad was four years old. His beautiful, healthy eighty-five-year-old wife, Corina Monrovia, is a retired multifaceted professor of philosophy, an accomplished poet, and successful writer of novels. She had taught Brad philosophy and poetry during his freshman year of college.

Generally it took Brad about twenty minutes to drive to the professors' home, mostly along roads near the ocean. While he drove, Brad remembered how much the professor had affected his life. The picturesque drive provided the perfect atmosphere to reminisce about some of the wonderful bits of advice the professor had given to Brad.

His thoughts took him back to memories of his childhood, including cherished memories of the professor taking him to different animal sanctuaries and reserves several times when he was five and six years old. He would instruct Brad to carefully pet the adult animals first and then the babies. Brad remembered that his first real contacts with animals were with horses, lambs, pigs, goats, dogs, and cats. Additional visits included viewing birds, butterflies, bees, ants, and spiders. Occasionally when Brad would pet an animal or inspect an insect, the professor would whisper to him.

"Never be cruel to any living creature, and always protect them from harm." Then he would say, "This is kindness; this is love."

The Monrovia's oceanfront home is located on five acres of property in Mission Viejo. Two inland waterways cut through the property and make a perfect setting for what is also partly used as a nature and animal retreat. The rolling and hilly land is home to several horses, trumpeter swans, dogs, and cats, and two intelligent talking parrots. It is accented by numerous perennial flowering gardens. Brad's meetings have always taken place in the professor's large front yard. Brad met the professor near the entrance to a patio in the yard just as the professor was pouring himself a cup of tea.

"Good morning, Professor. Thank you for seeing me today."

"Good morning, Brad. It is always a pleasure to visit with you. I hear wonderful things about your scholastic achievements from my fellow teachers at the university. Please sit with me and have some tea. How can I help you today?"

"Sir, my final thesis for philosophy deals with the benefits of human wisdom regarding how much better off the United States and most of the world is today simply because of kindness to animals since the Animal Welfare Act of 2008. I am comfortable with the content that explains today's conditions, but I have had great difficulty dealing with my antipathy and emotions while researching the horrors that existed for all species of animal life until 2008. I see vivid, terrifying images in my dreams of animals being tortured while they scream and desperately fight to survive, just prior to being brutally killed in slaughterhouses.

"Also the cruel, blasé, heartless, nonchalant, and cavalier manner that hunters used to stalk and kill helpless deer is repulsive to me. I am now frightened by these nightmares that are more real than life, and by my overwhelming urges to find some way, even killing, to stop the animal killers. All the rational thought I have used when trying to persuade the incorrigible monsters in my dreams to stop the cruelty and killing has failed. The desire for personal revenge to satisfy my animosity is like a last resort.

"Professor, you have been my mentor for as long as I can remember, teaching me on many subjects, especially about the wisdom of being kind to all living creatures and the virtues of nonviolence. Please help me understand so I can regain the mental strength and composure I will need to stand in front of my classmates and make an oral presentation comparing the wonderful lives animals live today with the unthinkable conditions that existed until 2008."

The professor began a long, reassuring explanation.

"My son, you were fortunate to be raised in a nonviolent society. Your nightmares are about people not as fortunate as you who were raised in an atmosphere of violence, especially violence to animals. You inherited your parents' and ancestors' biological cells and have spent your life as a vegetarian, which means your mind and body are overwhelmingly filled with nurtured habits of kindness, love, and protection toward all living creatures.

"Throughout your life, I have tried to pass along and impress you with ancient words of wisdom related to the most important saying, which is 'protect and preserve the earth and all the creatures that dwell here.

"Do not condemn the people in your dreams who maintained the habitual inherited acts of consuming meat and condoning the cruelty and killing of animals that had existed just about everywhere for thousands of years. Eating meat was as natural as drinking water. Habits like that are very difficult to change.

"Until 2008, babies and adolescents in the United States were given no choice but to eat many foods containing meat. As children grew, they were fed many kinds of meats such as hot dogs, hamburgers, bacon, chicken, steak, and fish.

"Most children were completely unaware of where the food came from until well into their adolescence. The point is they ate meat because almost everyone in the United States ate meat. In my opinion, meat eaters subconsciously thought that was the way it had always been and always would be. Many of the hunters that sicken you in your dreams probably owned dogs and cats that they loved and cared for; but they did not feel the same way about the animals they were hunting.

"God's seeds of kindness, love, and nonviolence have always existed in the souls of all humans and animals. The hunters and meat eaters you abhor in your dreams are the same type of people as those who changed their ways and decided not to be a part of the atrocities.

"Many hunters of animals became protectors of animals. Individually and collectively they campaigned to convince thousands of active hunters and slaughterhouse workers to stop participating in the killing of animals.

"Surprisingly, compassionate ex-hunters and ex-meat eaters in America played an important role in helping to convince the United States Congress in 2008 to pass laws to remove meat from the food chain for humans and animals.

"Bradford, you could have been just like the people you loathe if you had been raised in the same environment—a world that placed great importance on eating meat, and hunting animals for food and sport.

"Only after the painstaking and gradual realization that animals, humans, and the earth must coexist—and each is equally important for the others to survive—did we arrive at the place we are today, which is our constant attempt to preserve and protect the lives of all of God's creatures.

"Beginning in February, 2007, consumer fears about the hazards of eating meat were dramatically enhanced by new information that was both provocative and frightening. Worldwide media reports finally substantiated many earlier accusations by disclosing evidence proving that consuming the dead flesh of animals contributed to or caused most human diseases. Even more terrifying was the fear of larger outbreaks of the dreaded Mad Cow disease that could have potentially killed hundreds of thousands of people in the United States.

"Almost immediately, millions of people in the United States stopped eating any type of meat. In March, 2007 large numbers of slaughterhouse workers around the world began to walk off the job. In November, 2007 the first large slaughterhouses in the United States began to shut down. The last slaughterhouses in the United States closed in June 2008."

"In all the world of Utopia there is no meat. There used to be. But now we cannot stand the thought of slaughterhouses. And in a population that is all educated, and at about the same level of physical refinement, it is practically impossible to find anyone who will hew a dead ox or pig. I can still remember as a boy the rejoicings over the closing of the last slaughterhouse."

H.G. Wells. A Modern Utopia

"On a large scale, cruelty gave way to kindness, and death gave way to life, so that today animals have the opportunity to live full, safe, and happy lives.

"The persons in your dreams are capable of feeling and expressing the same love and kindness you do. Try to dissuade them into taking a different path, the path of nonviolence. Bradford, our conversation reminds me of one of my favorite Hindu scriptures:

"He who sees that the lord of all is ever the same in all that is immortal in the field of mortality, he sees the truth. And when a man sees that the God in himself is the same God in all that is, he hurts not himself by hurting others. Then he goes, indeed, to the highest path.

"Bradford, when you have nightmares again, do not be hateful. Try to pass along these words that are thousands of years old, so all may understand as you have."

"Thank you, Professor. I think I will be all right now. Your kind wisdom is greatly appreciated. I will stay in touch with you."

The Professor gave Brad a short hug and bid him farewell.

Sunday evening Brad began to dream about his own cat and dogs being hunted by other heartless killers. He imagined people who he knew seeing their pets dragged off to slaughterhouses and brutally killed. When he awoke he immediately made several phone calls trying to warn his friends and neighbors. One of his neighbors told him he needed to stop his research because he was beginning to act crazy.

More then ever, Brad now realized that he had to take better control of his emotions. Thankfully, he thought, the days of humans killing animals and eating their flesh ended in 2008 in most countries. With some significant exceptions, the largest percentage of animals in the world are now protected and shielded from acts of cruelty or killing.

Now that he had gathered enough information about the gory details of a bygone era, he was happy to begin accumulating data for his first classroom presentation about the wonderful lives most animals in the world enjoy today in 2065.

"The beef industry has contributed to more American deaths than all the wars of this century, all natural disasters, and all automobile accidents combined. If beef is your idea of real food for real people, you'd better live real close to a real good hospital."

Neal D. Barnard M.D. Physicians Committee for Responsible Medicine, Washington, D.C.

Chapter Two

How Kindness to Animals
Has Changed the World

It was the first day of philosophy class presentations.

"Good morning, my name is Bradford Knox. The title of my presentation is: How Kindness to Animals Has Changed the World

"First we will evaluate how animals are treated in 2065 and how the quality of their lives has improved. Then we will evaluate some of the gains realized over the last fifty-seven years as a result of Americans removing meat from the food chain for humans and animals. This remarkable, incomparable change began with the Animal Welfare Act on September 1, 2008. Surprisingly, we now enjoy many residual benefits and our country has become far less violent and far more compassionate to all living creatures. Let me begin.

"Today, in America animals are cherished and protected by most people, and are special members of our nation. The no-kill laws put into effect in 2008 were intended to protect all animal life. They included provisions to implement birth control measures of spaying and neutering in order to humanely reduce, control, provide for, and protect the overall animal population. Within several months the new practices began to dramatically reduce the heavy overpopulation of most animals, especially dogs and cats.

"Since the elimination of all animal factory-farms and the continuous expanded nationwide effort of spaying and neutering for nearly fifty-seven years, the population of animals in the United States each year has been significantly reduced. The overall animal population has declined by approximately 74 percent from 2008 to 2065.

"During the last fifty seven years hundreds of new animal reserves and sanctuaries have been continually developed throughout the United States and are thriving. The main purpose and goal of creating the reserves and sanctuaries was to one day have the physical capabilities to provide safe haven for all wild animals in America. That goal was finally achieved in November of 2029.

"The gruesome sport of hunting, as well as the raising and killing of animals for their fur or other body parts, have been nearly nonexistent for over fifty-six years.

"Now animals receive many of the same health care benefits and modern hospital services that humans receive. There are 187 large state of the art animal hospitals in the United States. Highly skilled doctors and staff members are well paid to provide the finest technology and medicine for every species of animal.

"Animal hospitals, shelters, humane societies, reserves, and sanctuaries can no longer put animals to death unless they can convince a state official that the animal is either so critically ill or so severely injured that nothing else can be done to save its life.

L.A.P. Day (Love and Protection Day), the national holiday for animals in the United States, is celebrated each year on September 1 to commemorate the Animal Welfare Act of 2008 and to remind our citizens how important it is to love and protect all animal life. Many countries in the world have a similar holiday at different times of the year.

"This country and most of the world are now far safer and healthier for humans and animals to live in largely because of changes in our educational systems.

"Our goal was to use the most effective methods to help develop a permanent habit in our children of loving and protecting all animal life.

"The ancient theories that we began to teach in our education systems in 2007 planted the seeds of hope. By July 2007, all elementary schools in the United States were required to include classes on kindness to animals beginning in the third or fourth grade.

"In addition, our earliest childhood teachings incorporated the oriental concept of ahimsa (nonviolence), which expresses the sacredness of all life, a unity that includes even insects.

"I will now read to you two Hindu verses both of which were often read to students by our teachers and also recited by most students from third to eighth grade. Many of us used and referred to these verses throughout our school years and will continue to practice these beliefs for the remainder of our lives.

As long as human society continues to allow cows to be regularly killed in slaughterhouses, there cannot be any question of peace and prosperity.

A.C. Bhaktivedanta Swami Prabhupada

If we are to reach real peace in this world and if we are to carry on a real war against war, we shall have to begin with children; and if they grow up in their natural innocence, we won't have to struggle; we won't have to pass fruitless idle resolutions, but we shall go from love to love and peace to peace, until at last all the corners of the world are covered with that peace and love for which consciously or unconsciously the whole world is hungering."

Mahatma Gandhi

Brad continued, "For nearly six decades our children have been raised in a non-violent society. Our children have been raised as vegans. Every day they are exposed to nonviolence as a principle of peace and compassion. Every day they are reminded in some way to not kill.

"This love, compassion, and protection have had a huge impact, resulting in a society that commits far fewer acts of violence against animals and people.

"During the last fifty-seven years, the vast majority of our children have been taught by their families and educated in our schools to believe that animals are one of God's most glorious gifts to the world, all of which must be protected and cared for, and never harmed.

"For the last twenty-two years all states have added animal welfare courses to high school and college curricula. Now animal welfare degrees are sought by thousands of students who will be seeking the high-paying jobs that are now available for such graduates.

"For Americans, living in a nonviolent society has significantly contributed to a large reduction in every type of crime, especially severe felonies. The most dramatic reductions in crime when comparing 2064 with 2007 are that murder, rape, armed robbery, and domestic violence have been reduced by between 85 to 92 percent.

"The Nonviolence Act of 2009 forced writers, movie and radio producers, and the news media to refrain from using any type of violence in their productions. The restriction also applied to manufacturers of toys and games. The Nonviolence Act concluded that freedom of speech does not mean freedom to exhibit or promote any type of violence.

Mahatma Gandhi once said: "Liberty never meant the license to do anything at will."

"The proven methods we established in America have now been endorsed and instituted by many countries in the world. In today's world, most people believe we are all, animals and humans, of the same race and religion. We are all holy beings established in divinity itself. This is the reason sages have emphatically proclaimed again and again that it is necessary to love all existing lives as one's own. This belief played a large role in creating the practice of vegetarianism, as did the theory that there is little difference between the soul of an animal and that of a man, and that through reincarnation a human soul might enter the body of an animal.

"This ends my report for today. Tomorrow I will begin my presentation explaining how much the state of our health has improved. Thank you."

"As long as there are slaughterhouses, there will be battlefields. What I think about vivisection (operating on a live animal for the purpose of scientific research) is that if people admit that they have the right to take or endanger the life of living beings for the benefit of many, there will be no limit to their cruelty."

Leo Tolstoy, author

Chapter Three
How Bad Things Used to Be

That evening during dinner, Brad asked his father, Richard, to explain why it took thousands of years for humans to finally realize that eating animal flesh was so detrimental. Richard Knox answered, "The best way to answer your question is to look back at the state of violence toward animals and humans that existed in most of the world throughout history until 2008. Until then modern man was not much different psychologically than he was thousands of years ago. He was violent, greedy, and selfish, and was just the push of a button away from being completely destroyed by nuclear war. Never ending violence and decadence throughout the world made it impossible to have long lasting peace and harmony.

"The straw that finally broke the camel's back was the coincidence of several critical factors. First was the proof that diseased cells from the dead flesh of slaughtered animals were being nourished within the bodies of billions of meat eaters.

"Starting in December of 2006 were continuous reports of hundreds of people in the United States dying from the very mysterious new variant Creutzfeldt-Jakob disease, a brain eating affliction that experts said was the human version of BSE, bovine spongiform encephalopathy, or Mad Cow Disease. Because of a lack of regulation it was impossible to know to what extent the disease had entered and spread throughout the food chain.

"Evidence confirmed the transspecies link gave credence to the notion that the disease which had a long an undetermined incubation period would someday become much more wide spread.

"The worldwide horror about the Mad Cow Disease arose from the hideous nature of it. Over a prolonged and ghastly period, victims displayed involuntary movements and appeared insane. The theory was that many people became infected with the brain-wasting disease after eating beef from cows that had been fed brain and nerve tissue of infected animals.

"Meats were proven contributors to all major illnesses and countless deaths to humans as well as animals. Most Americans became convinced that eating dead animal flesh played a significant role in perpetuating a worldwide cycle of confusion, cruelty, disease, and death to humans and animals.

"Subsequently millions of people throughout the world began to finally realize that meat was so harmful to their health, and that cruelty to animals was so appalling, it made no sense to continue killing billions of animals for human consumption."

"Ending most cruelty to animals in the United States in 2008 was the first step toward setting an example of the benefits of kindness to humans and animals for the world to emulate and benefit from."

Just then Brad's mother, Laura, began serving dinner. It was a family favorite: salad, then vegetarian turkey and stuffing with a rice and bean soufflé, along with mashed potatoes and side dishes of broccoli and tomatoes. The family's three pets—Maggie, an English Springer spaniel; Heidi, a wire haired Dachshund; and Yogi, a Siamese cat—generally ate the same dinner food in the adjoining room.

Shortly after dinner, Brad decided to go to bed so he could be well rested for the next day's classroom presentation. Immediately after falling asleep he began to dream again. This time he found himself sitting at a dinner table with the hunter Mondo in a crowded restaurant.

Mondo was talking. "This is the only joint in town that serves rabbit food. That's why I thought you would like it."

"Good to see you again, Mondo. What do you have a taste for?"

"You tell me," said Mondo. "It all looks like it's already been eaten to me."

"How about a vegetarian Salisbury steak with mashed potatoes, vegetarian gravy, and sweet corn. Maybe for starters, pea soup with homemade buns and salad. For desert, homemade cherry pie?"

"Forget the salad," Mondo said, "and make sure to ask for a barf bag for me." While the meal was being prepared Brad decided to find out more about Mondo's life.

"So, Mondo, tell me: when did you start hunting animals?"

"Actually, my father began teaching me how to fish when I was five years old. Then when I was ten he taught me how to hunt pheasants. I began deer hunting with my father when I was twelve. Have you ever hunted?"

"No, when I was a child there was no such thing as hunting, except for those who broke the law."

"Did you ever eat meat?" asked Mondo.

"No."

"What about chicken or fish?"

"No."

"How about baby food? You must have eaten meat in your baby food!"

Brad shook his head. "For my entire life it has been against the law to buy, sell, or eat food that contains any type of animal meat. My parents fed me baby food that was composed of much healthier ingredients then meat. My vegan form of eating began at birth and will continue for the rest of my life."

"You're not bullshitting me now? What you have said is the truth?"

"Correct. What I have said is the truth. I was raised in an entirely different environment than you. I have never seen butchered meat of any kind, and no one I know would risk being caught with meat in his or her possession. My parents never ate meat; and my grandparents who lived many years before 2008 did not eat meat.

"My true feeling is that if I lived in the same type of society you were raised in I would most likely eat meat and would probably hunt and kill animals. Mondo, if you had been raised in the society I live in you would not have been a hunter and you would have never eaten meat."

"So what's the catch?" Mondo asked. "Why did everyone stop eating meat?"

"Funny you should ask. I am currently doing a presentation for my philosophy class explaining how much better off the world is because of kindness to animals. In order to answer your question I will explain some of the important points that are in my presentation.

"During your time in history, especially between 1990 and 2008, many animal rights organizations began to find ways, through massive member support, to make millions of people aware of the cruelty toward and needless killing of animals. Most of the adult population in the United States became convinced that meat was extremely harmful to their health, and that cruelty to animals was senseless.

"Congress was finally persuaded to institute new animal rights laws in 2008. The new laws forbade any type of cruelty to animals including hunting, killing, slaughtering, laboratory experimentation, and consumption of any type of meat.

"In 2007 all elementary schools throughout the United States made it mandatory to include classes for children beginning in the third or fourth grade teaching them the importance of nonviolence and the importance of kindness to animals and people."

Mondo spoke up. "I find it hard to imagine that this will all happen. Hunters must have been extremely opposed to the passage of the laws you say will take effect in 2008."

"During the early stages of change, prior to 2008, most hunters did fight vigorously to maintain their rights to hunt and kill animals," agreed Brad. "However, hunters gradually became more considerate and sympathetic toward the arguments in favor of protection, kindness, and love for animal life. Most rational hunters began to realize that there was no real benefit in killing animals. Their motivation to kill helpless animals gave way to a feeling of compassion and protection, and the numbers of hunters began to decrease rapidly.

"Religious books promoting ancient beliefs about protecting animals became popular and were sold in book stores throughout the United States. They were advertised often by every form of media available. Pamphlets containing inspirational sayings were often handed out to hunters by animal rights protesters, especially just prior to and during hunting seasons. Let me recite two of the Hindu sayings:

Goodness is never one with the minds of these two: One who wields a weapon and one who feasts on a creature's flesh.

When an individual's consciousness lifts and expands, he or she will abhor violence and not be able to even digest the meat, fish, or fowl he was formerly consuming. India's greatest saints have confirmed that one cannot consume meat and live a peaceful, harmonious life."

Brad paused to look at Mondo and noticed that Mondo seemed somewhat transfixed and was glaring off into space.

"So Mondo, any thoughts about what I just said?"

"You made me think about my childhood and how different our lives have been. My true gut feeling is that I never really enjoyed killing animals. Hunting was just something most of my family and friends often did. Actually it was very difficult for me emotionally to kill the first several deer, and then I slowly became numb to it all. Many times I wondered why I was killing a helpless, defenseless animal that had caused me no harm."

"Mondo, unlike yours, my childhood memories are filled with many teachings taken from ancient beliefs, which stressed the importance of kindness to all living creatures. My parents made certain that their Hindu philosopher, Doctor Monrovia, would begin teaching me about the value of kindness to animals when I was four years old. He is still my advisor to this day. All through grammar school, high school, and college, I and most of my classmates were taught to be kind to all animals and to protect them from any type of harm.

"Mondo, please consider reading the Tirukural written about 2200 years ago. This ethical masterpiece was written by the South Indian sage Tiruvalluvar. The author masterfully and eloquently expresses an ageless form of wisdom, and truth. There are many verses within the Tirukural that convincingly explain why it is much wiser to take the path of nonviolence."

"Ok, I'll give it a whirl, even though this all sounds like some kind of unrealistic fairy tale."

Mondo began to eat his vegetarian meal. He slugged the food down so fast it was amazing he was able to breathe at the same time. "That was absolutely delicious!" he said. "Thanks for the recommendation!"

"I am pleased you enjoyed it. Where I live the food tastes even better and there are many more choices."

"You have an entertaining, story-telling imagination," replied Mondo.

Brad responded, "Please remember if you must go out hunting again, especially when you are aiming at a helpless deer, that only a heartless person would kill a harmless, innocent animal. You can glorify the activity and rationalize the necessity all you want, but the truth is there is nothing good about killing."

Just then the dream ended again. Brad hoped that he could continue the dream some other time because he was very curious about the way animals used to be treated in Mondo's world.

"The time will come when men such as I will look upon the murder of animals as they now look on the murder of men."

Leonardo da Vinci, artist and scientist

Chapter Four
More Benefits from Protecting Animals

Brad felt invigorated and positive as he stood before his classmates to present his next report.

"Good morning, everyone. Today I will talk about some of the many health benefits for humans and animals directly related to eating non-meat foods. I will also explain why, in my opinion, no single decision by individuals or a race has caused a more dramatic improvement in our planetary ecology than the decision to not eat animal flesh. Finally, I will evaluate and discuss the spiritual consciousness today, and how our children and adults have benefited because of vegetarian foods.

"Food is the source of the body's chemistry; what we ingest affects our consciousness and emotions. If one wants to live in a higher consciousness—in peace, happiness, and love for all creatures—then one cannot eat meat, fish, or fowl. By ingesting the grosser chemistries of animal foods, one introduces into the body and mind anger, jealousy, fear, anxiety, suspicion, and a terrible fear of death.

"Religious beliefs shared by millions of people also insist that if you involve yourself in the cruel cycle of inflicting injury, pain and death—even indirectly by eating the flesh of creatures—then you will in the future experience an equal measure of the suffering you caused.

"In the United States, eating plant-based foods now protects humans from the day they're born until their projected life span of 95 to 110 years for men and women. We expect that many of our citizens will live happy, healthy lives until they are at least 115 to 125 years old. These calculations result from monitoring the lives of nearly forty-five million Americans born between 1960 and 1970 who are alive and well today.

"Meat eaters used to clog up their arteries with a diet loaded with animal fat, putting themselves at great risk for the killers of the western world, heart attack and stroke. Animal meat is high in sodium, which causes the blood to retain water; it also causes plaque to build up in the arteries, restricting the flow of blood. Combine these problems and you have the recipe for a disease that afflicted about fifty million Americans yearly between 1990 and 2007, high blood pressure. Now our population enjoys vegetarian foods that naturally clear out artery plaque buildup, which often used to require the expensive and widespread procedure of angioplasty.

"Studies concluded in 2064 proved that most animals lived considerably longer and much healthier lives due to eating non-meat foods. Prior to 2008 the average life span for meat eating dogs, depending on their size and breed, ranged between nine to thirteen years. The average life span for meat eating cats ranged between ten to fifteen years. In 2064 the average life span for non-meat eating dogs was twenty one to twenty eight years and for cats twenty four to thirty years.

"For hundreds of years, meat was the primary choice of food made by most people in the western world, especially in America. Between 2000 and 2007 a major expansion in health food stores happened, largely due to the rapidly growing demand for vegetarian substitutes for all meats, including chicken and fish. It became the in thing to do.

"Slogans such as 'vegetarians live longer, look better, are healthier' and 'kindness to animals is cool' swept across the United States. Now in 2065 thousands of health food supermarkets are found around the world.

"Today, because of fifty-seven years of our vegetarian diet, most diseases such as cancers, heart disease, strokes, and diabetes has been significantly reduced. In essence we did not cure these diseases, but rather we removed the root causes.

"The remarkable and inconceivable improvement in health during the last six decades is overwhelmingly the result of eliminating chemically preserved, decayed, disease-tainted animal flesh from the food chain. Simultaneously our citizens have benefited immensely by strengthening their bodies' immune systems.

"In the United States before 2008 about 25 million pounds of antibiotics were fed every year to livestock for growth promotion and disease prevention, almost eight times the amount given to humans to treat disease, not so much to treat infection, but to make the animals grow faster on less feed. Though perfectly legal, the practice had the effect of promoting the selection of antibiotic-resistant bacteria. Some of the bacteria caused human diseases that physicians were finding very difficult to treat. The practice added to a general worldwide crisis of drug-resistant disease. Each year in the 1990s about 60,000 Americans died because their medications were ineffective in combating bacterial strains.

"In 1995, approximately 683,000 Americans died prematurely as a result of atherosclerosis-related diseases. In other words, they died largely as a result of their meat-eating ways. Those figures represented 29 percent of all deaths that year.

"Though osteoporosis was a disease of calcium deficiency, it was not usually caused by low calcium intake. The primary cause of the once-dreaded bone disorder was too much protein in the diet. Excess protein was leaching calcium from the bones of American meat eaters. Our health experts knew that African Bantu women on low-protein diets take in a third of the United States recommended daily allowance of calcium. Many of these women often bear as many as nine children during their lifetime and breast-feed them for two years. They never have calcium deficiency and never break a bone. The typical meat-eating American before 2008 was eating about five times as much protein as needed.

"Tests performed between 1990 and 2000 revealed that those who ate dead animal flesh were far more likely to contract cancer than those eating vegetarian foods. The risk of contracting breast cancer was almost four times greater for women who ate meat daily compared to those who ate it less than once a week.

"Adult-onset diabetes was irrefutably linked to fat in the diet. Researchers found that when diabetics ate low-fat, high-fiber vegetarian foods, they were often able to reduce or even eliminate their insulin dosages. Tragically, as people around the world increasingly adopted meat-based diets, their incidences of diabetes, which leads to aggressive atherosclerosis, gangrene, blindness, and kidney failure, rose dramatically.

"In 1995 there were approximately 125 medical schools in the United States; only 30 required their students to take a course in nutrition. The average nutrition training received by the average U.S. physician during four years in school was only a few hours. Therefore, doctors in the United States were ill equipped to advise their patients to minimize certain foods, such as meat, that contained excessive amounts of cholesterol and were known contributors to heart attacks.

"Another way to show a link between diseases and diet is to look at living populations that ate differently in the world prior to 2008. Western doctors who practiced in eastern areas of the world where the people subsisted primarily on plant foods quickly realized that their patients had much lower percentages, and in some cases none of the health problems and deadly diseases that plagued the west, illnesses such as heart disease, gallstones, appendicitis, varicose veins, hemorrhoids, colorectal cancer, diverticulosis, and hiatal hernias."

"Studies done in 2003 revealed that eating meat dramatically raised the risk of heart attack. Heart attack was once the most common cause of death in the United States, killing one person every forty-five seconds.

"A meat eater's risk of death from heart attack was 50 percent. Even when modern technology saved heart patience lives millions of people were still left with congestive heart failure as a result of damaged hearts not able to circulate blood to the rest of their body adequately. This resulted in fluid build-up and organ damage.

"In 2001 in the United States nearly 5 million people lived with congestive heart failure, and about 550,000 new cases cropped up every year. The disease was the leading cause of hospitalization among the elderly and hospital bills attributed to congestive heart failure came to $19 billion per year.

"During the period between 1990 and 2008, many more doctors recommended vegetarian foods and regular exercise for heart patients, proving heart disease did not have to be a death sentence or mean a life of cholesterol-lowering drugs and bypass surgery.

"Bypass surgery required that a person's rib cage be opened, their heart stopped, and that their body be hooked up to an external pumping machine so an artery or vein from some other part of their body could be removed and grafted as a replacement blood vessel to their heart. Memory, language ability and spatial orientation were still impaired in 10 to 50 percent of bypass patients six months later. For some people the side effects never went away. Many required a second operation.

"Today in 2065 because of fifty-seven years of removing meat from the food chain, the risk of death from heart attack is 6 percent.

"The complex carbohydrates, antioxidants, vitamins, minerals, and fiber in plant-based foods guard against disease. Also, the more plant foods you eat, the less room you have for the animal foods that clog arteries with cholesterol, strain kidneys with excess protein, and burden the heart with saturated fat.

"During the 1990s the American Dietetic Association acknowledged a relationship between a vegetarian diet and reduced risk of coronary artery disease, hypertension, diabetes, obesity, and certain types of cancer. In 2003 a small but influential Canadian study found that a vegetarian diet, including soy, reduced cholesterol levels by about as much as widely used drugs.

"The second leading cause of death among men in 1998 was prostate cancer. This was not just an inevitable outcome of getting old; it was a result of a lifetime of eating animal fats. Animal fats stimulate the production of male hormones, which in turn help prostate cancer cells to grow.

"Vegetarians are less susceptible to all the major diseases that once afflicted humanity, and thus live longer, healthier, and more productive lives. They have fewer physical complaints, less frequent visits to the doctor, fewer dental problems, and smaller medical bills. Their immune systems are stronger, their bodies are purer and more refined, and their skin is more beautiful. All of this, plus the benefit of having unlimited choices of vegetarian foods that taste delicious.

"That ends my presentation for today. Tomorrow we will take a close look at how well farmers in the United States are doing, especially on land that used to be used for cattle farming."

"Our task must be to free ourselves by widening our circle of compassion to embrace all living creatures and the whole of nature and its beauty. Nothing will benefit human health and increase chances of survival for life on earth as much as the evolution to a vegetarian diet."

Albert Einstein, physicist, Nobel Prize winner 1921

Chapter Five

More Fertile Land,
More Prosperous Farmers

The following morning Brad was anxious to present a considerable amount of information proving how much better off farmers are now compared to before 2008.

"Today in 2065, most of the world's massive hunger problems have been solved. In 2001 approximately twenty million people worldwide died as a result of malnutrition, one child every 2.3 seconds. In 2064 less than fifty thousand deaths resulted from starvation, mostly in remote villages throughout Africa and India. Prior to 2008, raising livestock for meat was a very inefficient way of generating food. Pound for pound, far more resources were expended to produce meat than to produce grains, fruits, and vegetables. For example, more then half of all the water used in the United States was consumed in livestock production. While twenty-five gallons of water are enough to produce a pound of wheat, five thousand gallons were needed to produce a pound of California beef. The same five thousand gallons of water can now produce two hundred pounds of wheat.

"Meat eating was devouring oil reserves at an alarming rate. It used to take nearly seventy-eight calories of fossil fuel energy (from oil, natural gas, etc.) to produce one calorie of beef protein and only two calories of fossil fuel energy to produce one calorie of soybean protein. If we had not stopped meat consumption in the United States in 2008, and if every human had eaten a meat-centered diet, the world's known oil reserves would have lasted about 13 years. Now in 2065, if most of the people living in meat eating countries in the world can soon be persuaded to begin following our non-meat-eating ways, these same oil reserves could last 260 years.

"Studies were often performed on the effects of chemicals in meat. Unknown to most meat eaters, the United States produced meat containing dangerously high quantities of deadly pesticides, and 99 percent of U.S. mother's milk contained significant levels of DDT.

"Contamination of breast milk in meat-eating mothers, due to chlorinated hydrocarbon pesticides in animal products, was found to be thirty-five times higher than in vegetarian mothers. Today in 2065 because of the 2007 NCP (No Chemical Pesticides) Act, zero percent of U.S. vegetarian mothers' milk contains DDT.

"Now farmers are far more prosperous because farmland has not been used to feed cattle for slaughter for nearly fifty-seven years. In 2001 about 56 percent of all U.S. farmland was devoted to beef production; to produce each pound of beef required sixteen pounds of edible grain and soybeans. Much of that same farmland is now used to produce vast amounts of corn, wheat, soybeans, fruits and vegetables for human consumption.

"Another example is how our potato farmers that used to be cattle farmers are prospering. Farmers that once produced 250 pounds of beef per acre now utilize their land to produce 40,000 pounds of potatoes per acre. The huge increase worldwide in the farmer's production and distribution of natural foods has just about eliminated starvation.

"Soybean farmers have enjoyed a major increase in sales because of the huge demand for soymilks and a large variety of soy-based foods. Textured vegetable protein and tofu had replaced many animal meat dishes such as hamburgers, steaks, chicken, pork, and fish.

"The No Chemical Pesticides Act also legislated that no farmland could be sprayed with harmful chemicals. Instead, beginning in 2007 highly concentrated mixtures of organically grown vegetable-based products such as garlic and pepper were developed and sprayed over all U.S. cropland. These new procedures for producing pure organically grown foods were very successful at repelling insects without killing them. The procedure immediately began removing harmful chemicals from all farm produce.

"Trees, especially old-growth forests, are essential to the survival of the planet. Their destruction was a major cause of global warming and topsoil loss. Meat eating was the number one driving force behind the destruction of those forests.

"By 2001 the years of huge continuous destruction had resulted in the clearing of about 260 million acres of U.S. forest for cropland to produce the meat-centered American diet. To produce each quarter pound of rainforest beef required the consumption of 55 square feet of tropical rainforest. By 2001 about 75 percent of all U.S. topsoil had been lost. Eighty-five percent of that loss was directly related to livestock raising.

"During the same period, to keep up with U.S. consumption, approximately 300 million pounds of meat was imported annually from Central and South America. Those economic incentives impelled those nations to cut down their forests to make more pastureland for animals. Another devastating result of deforestation was the loss of plant and animal species. Between 1991 and 2001 nearly a thousand species were eliminated each year.

"Prior to 2008, the escalating loss of species, the destruction of ancient rainforests to create pastureland for livestock, the loss of topsoil, and the increase of impurities in water and air were all traced back to the single fact of meat in the human diet.

"In 2008 mother earth began to slowly lick her wounds. Now most of the problematic trends have been reversed and have been in a slow constant remission.

"In our world today, because of fifty-seven years of not killing animals to consume meat, most countries comprised of people that do not eat meat have much healthier rejuvenated land.

"In 2011 the temperature of the earth stopped rising. Global warming, also referred to as the greenhouse effect, was caused primarily by carbon dioxide emissions from burning fossil fuels, such as oil and natural gas. Prior to 2008, three times more fossil fuels were burned to produce a meat-centered diet compared to a meat-free diet. Currently in 2065, because of nearly fifty-seven years of billions of people around the world not eating meat, global temperatures have dropped significantly and the threat of higher temperatures has vastly diminished.

"Thank you for listening to my presentation today. Tomorrow my subject will be the incredible abilities of service and companion animals, focusing on the benefits they provide to handicapped and non-handicapped people."

That evening Brad met Alyssa at Vincenzo's Italian Restaurant in Laguna Niguel. Brad planned to propose to Alyssa and present her with an engagement ring, so the evening needed to be as special as possible. They each drank a few glasses of wine and began eating a delicious meal. Then they spent most of the evening joking, laughing, and reminiscing about memories of their childhood days. As desert was being served, Brad wanted to begin expressing his feelings for Alyssa. When she returned from a visit to the ladies room Brad said to her, "I should wear an oxygen mask when I see you because you are breathtaking."

Alyssa responded, "Save your breath for when we are alone, you naughty boy."

"Alyssa, there is something I have wanted to say to you for quite a while, and I thought tonight might be an appropriate time."

"You're going to tell me one of your silly jokes, right?" Alyssa asked.

"This will not be a joke, even though it may sound a little corny."

"Okay, I'm ready. Go ahead."

"For a long time I have tried to put into words what it is that is so special about you, and why you are so important to me," Brad began. "We have spent many hours together discussing our opinions on many subjects. I remember the day we spent together last summer when we walked on the beach just before dawn. If you recall, we ate breakfast while we watched the sun's brightly shining rays slowly light up the ocean and were spellbound watching two rainbows that suddenly appeared. It was a windy day and there was a light misty rain that seemed to accentuate the fragrances from nearby flowering gardens.

"If my memory is correct we walked near the ocean for a few hours, and then drove to a large animal sanctuary. We admired many species of animals and their offspring. I remember thinking that no animal on earth has more natural peerless beauty then the Black Panther we saw whose majestic glowing eyes seemed to stare right through us. At dusk we sat on the beach to watch the red sun as it seemed to slowly disappear into the blue, windswept waves of the ocean.

"That was just a small example of the unparalleled beauty of nature, a beauty that has existed for millions of years. Alyssa, if God had decided to capture a small portion of all the beauty that nature has to offer and manifest that beauty into the form of a human, that person would look just like you. God must have been thinking of this beauty when you were created. You are one of God's most alluring magnificent productions."

Alyssa and Brad stared at each other for a moment. Alyssa could think of nothing to say in response.

Brad continued, "Therefore, because you are the most beautiful, most generous, kindest, funniest, and most intelligent person I will ever know, it is with nervous apprehensive pleasure that I ask you to accept this ring as my proposal of marriage."

Now Alyssa could not hold back her emotions. With a big smile and tears in her eyes, she affectionately hugged Brad as she put the ring on her finger. "Bradford! you sneak! The ring is beautiful, and you already know you are the person I want to spend the rest of this life with—and beyond, I hope. My answer to your proposal is a very big yes!" They hugged and exchanged a few short kisses then enthusiastically talked about wedding plans while they slowly finished their dessert.

After spending the next few hours with Alyssa at her home Brad said goodnight and began a twenty minute drive to his home. He began thinking how nice it would be to get home and have a quiet, sound sleep. Shortly after arriving home Brad began reading the newspaper in bed and then fell to sleep in about fifteen minutes. Unfortunately, halfway through the night his peaceful rest was interrupted by the same old nightmares and the pleasant sleep changed to horrible mind flashes of animals being tortured again.

As the dream continued, he somehow found himself at sunup standing in a woods filled with deer that were about to be hunted. The most bizarre part of the dream was that Brad had become a marksman with a high-powered rifle in his hand. This new found talent combined with his deep-rooted compassion for all animal life now made him sense the urgent necessity to do whatever it would take to prevent the deer from being killed.

The next scene in the dream revealed Brad beginning to aim his rifle at a hunter and lining up the sight. Then suddenly he realized that he could not pull the trigger. It was not in his nature to kill. He realized he would have to do something else to protect the deer. The only thing he could think of was to start firing his rifle in the air hoping to scare off as many deer as possible. He pointed the rifle to the sky and began firing indiscriminately, which caused the deer to scatter rapidly. The hunters were also alarmed and confused by the gunfire and retreated quickly. During the confusion, Brad ran inside a nearby barn and tried to hide in a hayloft. He listened to the sounds of commotion for about thirty minutes, then suddenly everything seemed to quiet down. When it looked and seemed like the coast was clear, Brad began to sneak out of the barn. Just then large floodlights were flashed at him that made him stop abruptly.

A voice yelled out, "You are surrounded by police. We have guns pointed at you! Lay your rifle on the ground, and then put your hands behind your head."

Just then Brad woke up from the dream, shaking and sweating profusely. He had never known the feeling of a momentary desire to kill, or the fear from almost being killed, and it sickened him. Even more frightening was that the dream seemed way too real.

Chapter Six
Great Companions, Wonderful Helpers

Brad now realized that the nightmares were not going to go away. He had to develop a mental toughness to deal with the anguish associated with his project. Before he began the next formal presentation, he decided to read a passage to his classmates from his reference material that he hoped would give him a chance to clear his mind of the horrors from the previous night's dream.

"Good morning. Before I begin my talk today, let me read to you one of my favorite Hindu passages.

"What is the good way? It is the path that reflects on how it may avoid killing any living creature. Refrain from taking precious life from any living being.

"Thank you now let me begin today's presentation.

"Because of animals the lives of handicapped people have greatly improved.

"The Americans with Disabilities Act (ADA), enacted in 1990, increased the training of service animals, mostly dogs, to help the disabled. The continuous success that has continued of many animal training organizations and individuals has made it obvious that animals can perform amazing services for handicapped people.

"These animals are allowed to join and assist their owners in buses, taxicabs, and trains, and to doctors' offices, stores, work, and just about every other place the general public is welcome. They are able to perform many tasks. A service animal can carry and pick up items, guide a person with impaired vision, or alert a person with impaired hearing to the presence of people, the smell of smoke, or the sound of a fire alarm or telephone.

"New and expanded programs of animals helping people began after legislation was sent to and passed by congress in October of 2008.

"Since 2010 several thousand licensed training schools that specialize in service animal care have been developed in the United States and around the world, supported by large financial subsidies from the federal government, plus donations from corporations and private individuals. These multipurpose schools now offer every level of affordable assistance to needy individuals.

"Now in 2065, millions of service animals worldwide assist and care for handicapped people, and give that special love and devotion so many handicapped people rely on and appreciate immensely.

"For handicapped senior citizens, Medicare expanded benefit coverage pays for most expenses related to specialized assistance animal training that is provided by licensed schools or individuals.

"To obtain and maintain a license, schools and individuals who train or handle animals must sign a pledge of kindness agreement that outlines how all animals must be treated. Violations of treatment standards can result in a loss of license plus substantial fines or imprisonment, depending on the offense."

"Animals should be treated with kindness at all times. Although a service animal must be skillful and consistent, how you accomplish that goal is significant. Animals need to be constantly rewarded with praise, food treats, given free time to lounge and play, and take leisure walks with their handlers often.

"In order to develop relationships that provide meaningful, health-enhancing, social support, a person must first meet other people. Studies beginning back in 1991 have confirmed that dogs and cats expose their owners to healthy encounters with strangers, facilitate interaction among individuals previously unacquainted, and help establish trust among the newly acquainted. Animals often become the antidote for human anonymity and have helped people build friendships.

"Thank you for listening to me today. Tomorrow, the subject of my final presentation will be Disease, Cruelty, and Death to Animals Prior to 2008."

Chapter Seven
Before We Knew We Really Cared

"Today's presentation, 'Disease, Cruelty, and Death to Animals Prior to 2008, is based on information obtained from reference materials concerning the plight of animals mostly from 1850 until and through 2007. A desire to end that abominable cruelty to animals was the main reason so many humans adopted a vegetarian diet.

"For many years just about every living species of animal was used in grisly, torturous laboratory experiments. Healthy animals were often used like live pin cushions, causing great pain and suffering, and their bodies were often ripped apart during a variety of different experiments.

"Tests ranged from injecting animals with every kind of drug, even cocaine and heroin, to the painful and often deadly procedures of inserting electrical probes into every orifice of the animal's bodies. Testing the effects of chemicals caused many animals to go blind or deaf, or to suffer from chemical burns to their skin, leading to a horrible, painful death.

"In most factory-farms a percentage of the animals became sick or crippled. The industry called them 'downers.' Federal laws did not protect them. Downers were dealt with in the most convenient way. Veterinary care was not wasted on them. If unable to walk, a downer was often dragged by chains or pushed with a tractor or forklift to slaughter. Some of these animals were left to starve or freeze to death.

"The Humane Slaughter Act that existed until 2008 required that animals be rendered unconscious with one swift application of a stunning device before slaughter. In reality that requirement was often not adhered to.

"Conveyor lines were pushed to breakneck speeds, frequently causing cattle, pigs, horses, and sheep to be shackled and throats slit without first being stunned. Animals were often skinned, boiled, and butchered alive.

"Most dairy cows lived with unnaturally swelled and sensitive udders, and most were never allowed out of their stalls. They were milked up to three times a day and kept pregnant nearly all of their abbreviated lives. A female cow's young were taken from her almost immediately after birth. The sole purpose for the cow's life was to be bred, fed, medicated, inseminated, and manipulated to achieve maximum milk production at minimum cost.

"A male calf experienced even harsher measures. If he was not immediately slaughtered, a newborn calf was likely taken to a veal factory. There he was locked up in a stall and chained by his neck to prevent him from turning around for his entire life. Sounds like fun. He was fed a special diet without iron or roughage. Then he was injected with antibiotics and hormones to keep him alive and to make him grow. He was kept in darkness except for feeding time. The result was a grown animal with flesh as tender and milky white as a newborn's.

"Bulls that were castrated were much easier to handle than those who were not. Their meat was also more marketable. There were three castration methods, two of which shut off the blood supply so that the testicles either were reabsorbed into the animal's body or simply fell away after a couple of weeks. In a third method, the scrotum was cut so that the testicles could be pulled out. Anesthesia was rarely given before any of these procedures, and sometimes operations were botched. The cruel procedures caused unnecessary pain and suffering and to often resulted in premature death.

"Animal agriculture routinely mutilated farm animals for its own convenience. Debeaking, branding, castration, ear notching, wing and comb removal, dehorning, teeth clipping and tail and toe docking were ever present tasks on farms and ranches. Not by veterinarians, but ranch and farm hands, who learned on the job how to perform the surgeries and procedures using restraint only, no anesthesia.

"Factory hens were forced to live in rows of cages stacked four high, by the thousands. Each hen was confined to about 48 square inches of space. After months of confinement, necks would be covered with blisters; wings bare, combs bloody, feet torn, and eyes and ears infected.

"When these hens became what the industry referred to as 'spent,' producers would truck the mutilated birds, often long distances, to slaughter. Or they would gas them, or grind them up while still alive, to be used as feed for the next flock. Most other birds were then hung on conveyor belts, terrified and screaming, as they began their journey through the final stages of their lives, including a low-voltage stunning and a throat-slitting. Nearly all commercial chickens died during bleed-out after a circular blade severed their necks. Poultry workers, who typically made the same movement up to twenty thousand times a day, suffered repetitive stress disorders at sixteen times the national average.

"Egg producers considered male chicks a liability. Chick sexers would divert them for expedient deaths. Humane methods were not required by any law. Most often, the little ones, chirping wildly for their mothers, were dumped into trash bins to die by crushing, suffocation, starvation, or exposure.

"Imagine the joy most families experienced on Thanksgiving, digging into the delicious dead flesh of a turkey. What the eager meat eaters did not realize or necessarily care about was that most of the turkeys were selectively bred for the kill. Their overgrown, huge breasts made it impossible for them to accomplish the sex act on their own, so the industry had to artificially inseminate them.

"The job was nearly as dehumanizing for the workers as it was for the tortured breeder birds that were essentially raped once or twice a week for twelve to sixteen months until the pleasant procedure of slaughter. How was that for kindness, especially so most Americans could properly celebrate the spirit of Thanksgiving. Happy holiday!!

"To produce foie gras, male ducks were force-fed six to seven pounds of grain three times a day with an air-driven feeder tube. The torturous process went on for twenty-eight days until the ducks' livers, from which the pate was made, bloated to six to twelve times their normal size. About 10 per cent of the ducks did not make it to slaughter. They died when their stomachs burst.

"In nature, swine avoid filth and will trek and root over 9 miles in a night. Before 2008 most factory internment provided a breeding sow cold straw less floors, noxious filth, deafening noise, and a space barely bigger than her body. The highly intelligent creature was often driven insane as she endured repeated pregnancies via artificial insemination. Her body was pinned in place to expose her teats to her piglets. When her productive capacity declined she was sent to a slaughterhouse.

"In 1995, massive pork operations in North Carolina created twenty-five hundred open cesspools of hog manure. That summer, university studies estimated that half of the cesspools were leaking contaminants into the groundwater. In the same summer at least five cesspool lagoons broke open, letting loose tens of millions of gallons of hog urine and feces into rivers and onto neighboring farmland.

"As hog feces and urine collected in giant cesspools around factory-farms, the sludge was broken down naturally by bacterial digestion. Hazardous nitrogen was eliminated, but in the process it was converted into ammonia gas. Every time it rained, excess phosphorous and nitrogen from the animals' urine and feces seeped into the waterways, causing algae blooms to spread. With subsequent rainfalls, the ammonia was returned to the earth, polluting rivers and streams. No mechanical method of retrieval existed to clean the contaminants; only nature could purify the land again. As a matter of fact, nature's cleanup is probably still going on today in 2065.

"During this same period, waste from livestock in the United States amounted to 130 times the waste produced by people. Large amounts of animal feces and urine, which should have been categorized as hazardous industrial waste because of the bacteria, wormy parasites, and viruses they carried, continually ended up leaking into groundwater across the country.

"The slaughterhouse was the final stop for animals raised for their flesh. Animals were transported to their place of death in all weather conditions. When it was brutally cold, animals often would freeze right to the sides of trucks or become frozen in the urine and feces that would build up on truck floors. In hot weather heat stress killed many.

"It is hard to imagine the pain and terror described by those who witnessed what went on daily in any of the hundreds of slaughterhouses in the United States and other countries. Even worse, the workers inside also had to participate in the crimes of mayhem and murder. They were not on the job for long. Of all the occupations in the United States, slaughterhouse workers had the highest turnover rate, plus the highest rate of on-the-job-injury.

"People who had any type of contact with slaughterhouses could not help but be affected by what they saw and heard. Neighbors living nearby experienced the terrified, angry screams of the animals being led to slaughter. A major part of the horror inside a factory-farm was the noise. Hog factory workers often wore ear protection to ward off the sounds of squealing animals banging against their metal cages

"Often in the ghastly slaughterhouse, drains and sewers were backed up with guts and coagulated blood. Too often the pools that developed came up to workers' ankles. The muck often splashed up onto the animals, spreading contamination. Sometimes dismembered heads from the shackled animals were dragged through urine, feces, and blood. Employees were often kicked or bitten by struggling animals that were not properly stunned, and there were many incidents of workers being crushed by animals falling off the line.

"From 1990 to 2000, nearly all of the roughly eight billion animals slaughtered yearly for food in the United States were the product of swift-moving assembly-line systems incorporating dangerous methods of efficiency. Animal farms had been allowed to grow into a grim corporate monstrosity, the scale of which is hard to believe or even comprehend.

"Unknown by most Americans, slaughterhouses processed enormous numbers of animals each year. In the United States in the year 2000, over 650,000 animals were killed for meat every hour. The average American consumed in a seventy-two-year lifetime approximately 11 cattle, 3 lambs and sheep, 23 hogs, 45 turkeys, 1100 chickens, and 862 pounds of fish! Bon appetite!"

Brad set his notes aside and looked up at the students in the classroom. He noticed how quiet and still everyone was, and the many grim facial expressions. He paused for a few additional moments then continued.

"Starting in 2003 it was reported that every day on average 600 people in the United States died so suddenly from cardiac arrest that they did not even make it to the hospital. Of the victims, 90 per cent had two or more arteries narrowed by hardening of the arteries, a disease inexorably linked to a meat-based diet.

"Every year, on average, each meat-eating American became sick and approximately nine thousand people died from something they ate. That something was probably of animal origin.

"In 1982 hamburger sickness or E. coli poisoning was rare. By 2002 up to 5 percent of cows harbored the deadly bug. Every year as many as twenty thousand Americans got sick from E. coli contamination and nearly five hundred died from it. Milder symptoms ranged from diarrhea and abdominal cramps to destruction of red blood cells. Those who survived a serious bout could still become blind; suffer from seizures, kidney failure, or paralysis; or need to have some or all of their bowels removed.

"Merely one to ten microbes of E. coli in a hamburger could kill a child. It was up to consumers to neutralize pathogens with cooking. Two types of bacteria, campylobacter and salmonella, accounted for 80 percent of food-borne illnesses and 75 percent of the nine thousand deaths that occurred from meat and poultry yearly from 1994 to 2008. One hamburger could contain the meat of a hundred different cows from several different countries. One infected animal could contaminate sixteen tons of beef.

"Once the majority of meat-eating people in the world were convinced that every animal deserved the right to live, and also realized to a large degree that meat consumption included the risk of major health hazards, laws were finally enacted to protect all animal life. Then we began to prove as a nation that we could survive perfectly well and consume much healthier food without killing animals. I would like to leave you with one last thought. Let me recite another Hindu scripture written by Jnaneshvari that I first heard when I was a young boy and that I think of often.

He who experiences the whole of creation as his very own self, who sees everything around him as the limbs of his own body, although he appears like an ordinary man to others, I consider him to be truly blessed. Strive to experience this sense of unity with all things, to feel yourself in the universe and the universe in you. I'm telling you again and again: There is no greater experience than the awareness of oneness."

Brad slowly moved away from the podium and walked out of the room.

Chapter Eight
Stop Hunting - Start Protecting

Mondo Pacenti, an intelligent, rational person, was quite concerned about his meetings with Brad. He kept wondering how Brad seemed to show up out of nowhere like a surrealistic apparition, and why Brad thought it was so important to persuade Mondo not to hunt animals and not to eat meat. Even more confusing was trying to determine the real value and overall purpose of their meetings and discussions. Clearly, even if Mondo chose to put down his hunting rifles and stopped eating meat, the net result would be only one less hunter and one less meat eater. Left remaining would be millions of hunters still on the prowl and hundreds of millions of humans still consuming meat.

To help satisfy his curiosity, Mondo decided he would follow Brad's recommendation and visit the Chicago public library. There he obtained a copy of the Tirukural which he later realized was considered to be one of the world's greatest books of ethical scriptures written about 2200 years ago. It took Mondo a few days to read the verses in the Tirukural and it took several more days to consider and mentally absorb the ancient words of wisdom. The verses convincingly and eloquently express practical wisdom touching on all aspects of an ideal life.

Mondo began to realize that humans do not have the right to decide and select which animals will live and which will die no matter what the man-written Bible says. Mondo loved his dogs dearly and was most interested in the Hindu verses that strongly insinuate that all animals should be protected from any form of cruelty. Mondo began to also understand that when it comes to the feeling of genuine love and concern for the welfare of animals there is no difference between pets and wild animals.

Mondo had never experienced the wisdom from this type of philosophy and he could not help but be impressed. Many of the comments that Brad made to him obviously came from these same pages.

Soon after being enlightened by the religious scriptures, Mondo began thinking about his own youth and the hidden sorrow and pain he felt when he killed that first deer. He thought about how his father tried to console him and convince him that it was right and proper to hunt and kill animals and that the shock of killing would eventually wear off. Mondo remembered some highlights from books he had read that weighed the arguments for and against killing animals.

The most important point, which Mondo's father mentioned often, was that dead flesh from animals had been consumed for at least thousands of years and that scriptures in the Bible said it was okay. Hundreds of millions of families for over two thousands years had given thanks to God for the food he had provided, including the dead flesh of animals.

Mondo recalled more of the hunter's philosophy his father taught him to believe. In the beginning of recorded history animals attacked humans for food, so one of the initial and essential reasons for humans to kill animals was for survival. Furthermore, farmers for centuries experienced the many problems that could happen when certain species of animals were allowed to multiply unchecked. Significant amounts of productive farmland had been destroyed by animals, reducing production, increasing prices, and causing major safety hazards with large numbers of animals wandering everywhere.

In the later years of the nineteenth century, Americans relentlessly killed millions of wild animals. During that period many species of animals became extinct and many more were on the verge of extinction. At the beginning of the twentieth century, hunters took center stage and were largely responsible for instituting the correct hunting methods needed for conservation and more humane methods of killing animals.

Wild animals had been known to attack and maim or even kill farmer's cattle, pets, and sometimes even family members. This caused farmers to hunt and kill wild animals for safety as well as for food. When wild animal attacks continued to happen, additional hunters were often hired by the city or state to kill off the surplus of animals and bring the population under control.

More words of persuasion from his father explained that professional hunters have a code of ethics that expresses respect and gratitude to animals that they kill, and that hunters share an understanding to kill only as many animals as can be used for food or other products and for the sake of conservation.

The hunter's philosophy points out the hypocrisy of people who complain about hunters but at the same time buy meat that is packaged in fancy cans or boxes, without admitting to themselves that animals had to die for this to occur. Another area of hypocrisy is the huge fur business that is fueled by the demands of thousands of persons purchasing fur products while at the same time saying that they are opposed to hunting. Furthermore, meat eaters should never complain about the plight of hunters or slaughterhouse workers, since it is the meat eater who fuels the need and demand for killing animals.

Mondo vividly remembered when he was a teenager the discussions his father had with fellow hunters regarding the need to humanely control the overpopulation of deer. His father was aware that an overabundance of deer could cause major property damage; he had seen it happen.

While Mondo was trying to remember more reasons that his father had used to justify hunting and killing, a certain Hindu scripture suddenly flashed through his mind written by Yajur Veda Samhita.

You must not use your God-given body for killing God's creatures, whether they are human, animal or whatever.

Mondo now clearly realized that his father's beliefs were the result of the society he was raised in, and although he meant well, he was wrong.

Mondo could not help thinking that if he could live his life over he would rather live in the non-violent society that Brad says he is from. After considerable introspection Mondo was now sure that he could get along perfectly well without hunting and killing animals. He decided to make a concerted effort to try vegetarian foods and if feasible to change his eating habits so they would not include meat.

Even though Brad Knox insisted it all had to do with awareness and was not Mondo's fault, Mondo was deeply upset and had a personal feeling of guilt for cruelly killing hundreds of harmless animals.

World opinion in 1986 was already beginning to change significantly regarding the real value of killing animals and eating meat. Certainly in the United States there were plenty of non-meat foods to go around, and Brad had really convinced Mondo that eating meat was clearly unhealthy.

That evening Mondo told his wife he would no longer hunt, and that his five-year-old son Michael would be taught to love and protect all animals, beginning immediately. The more he thought about the subject the more convinced he became. He hoped that he could somehow be forgiven for his unawareness and ignorance while needlessly destroying the lives of so many precious animals. Mondo began to carry along with him various books filled with Hindu scriptures. He also made certain that his wife Mia and son Michael were carefully and vigorously indoctrinated into becoming vegetarians.

Mondo became convinced that in the big picture nature's creatures are all brothers and sisters and deserve the chance to live full and safe lives. The power and higher intelligence bestowed on man is suppose to be used to protect all animals insuring they have safe and peaceful lives, not to torture, kill and eat them. People should feel sadness and pity, not pleasure, at the prospect that millions of mostly helpless innocent creatures much like their own pets are ruthlessly killed either for food or for the pleasure of killing.

Whenever his hunter friends asked him why he stopped hunting, Mondo would simply reply, "I do not really find any value or enjoyment in killing animals. As a matter of fact, the thought now repulses me." He also recommended that his former hunting associates read Hindu scriptures and verses and seriously consider the merits of not killing any living creature.

Mondo would occasionally recite parts of the scriptures from memory. One of his favorites was written by Sage Yogaswami:

We are all of the same race and religion. We are holy beings established in Divinity itself. This truth can be understood only by those who have grasped it through the magical charm of a life of Dharma, which means one should never do to another which one regards as injurious to one's own self. Because of that, sages have emphatically proclaimed again and again that it is necessary to LOVE ALL EXISTING LIVES AS ONE'S OWN.

The next step for Mondo was to get rid of the large number of hunting books the family had collected over the years. Some were about the so-called merits and benefits of hunting. Other books described the latest fancy hunting equipment, and provide instructions for improving one's skill at killing animals.

So one evening after drinking several glasses of wine and becoming emotionally motivated by the sad memories of some of the many animals he had hunted and killed, Mondo gathered every book that related to hunting. He then dumped the books onto an open field behind his barn and began to burn them all. As the fire burned he picked up a folder from the front seat of his car filled with Hindu scriptures and verses. He began to read verses out loud written over two thousand years ago:

"What is the good way? It is the path that reflects on how it may avoid killing any living creature. Refrain from taking precious life from any living being. It is the principle of the pure in heart never to injure others. What is virtuous conduct? It is never destroying life, for killing leads to every other sin."

Mondo watched the fire burn and suddenly had an unsettling feeling when he recalled and recited another ominous verse that would haunt him for the rest of his life written by Shrimad Bhagavatam.

"Those that are ignorant of real dharma , one should never do to another which one regards as injurious to one's own self, and though wicked and haughty, account themselves virtuous, kill animals without feeling of remorse or fear of punishment. Further in their next lives, such sinful persons will be hunted, killed and eaten by the same creatures they have killed in this world."

Mondo was now quite intoxicated and decided to finish his loud recitations of scriptures by reciting a part of one final verse from the obscure Mansahara Parihasajalpita Stotram:

"Those who eat the flesh of other creatures are nothing less than gristle grinders, blood drinkers, muscle munchers, carcass crunchers and flesh feeders. Those who make their throats a garbage pit and their stomachs a graveyard. Mean, angry, loathsomely jealous, confused and beset by covetousness, who, without restraint would lie, deceive, kill or steal to solve immediate problems. They are flesh feeders loathsome to the Gods, but friendly to the asuras, a selfish aggressive supernatural being that become their Gods and Goddesses. The blood sucking monsters who inhabit Naraka, a sacred place for highly respected persons and deceptively have it decorated to look like the pitriloka, the after death world of the ancestors where average quality human souls dwell. To such beings the deluded meat eaters pay homage and prostrate while munching the succulent flesh off bones."

As the fire subsided and the books were reduced to ashes, Mondo wiped away wine from his chin and began thinking about Brad. He hoped that he would somehow meet him again so that he could thank him for guiding him into a new direction in life.

Chapter Nine

Choose Kindness and Life, Renounce Cruelty and Death

Now in 2065 major pressures are being imposed on the reduced number of meat-producing countries in the world. The huge reduction in the world's animal population and slaughterhouses has created additional problems of supply and demand. Most non-meat-eating countries in the western world have conformed and adopted the new techniques and principles of farm production and have benefited greatly from a huge increase in agricultural prosperity.

Unfortunately, there is still a significant demand for dead animal flesh in a number of countries such as China, Japan, Russia, several Asian countries, and all the countries of Africa. Repeated efforts from 2008 to 2065 by the United States have failed to persuade these meat eating countries to change their ways. In addition, a black market exists to satisfy the small percent of Americans who are willing to risk the consequences of breaking the law to satisfy their thirst for the manly sport of killing or the insatiable desire to consume chemically preserved dead decaying animal flesh.

Currently because so many countries have stopped killing animals for meat consumption and exportation, the motivation is much greater now for Africa to increase production to meet the demands of millions of people in several large countries that still eat meat. A percentage of hunters from around the world, including frustrated hunters from the United States who do not want to be caught breaking the law, are willing to pay exorbitant amounts of money to travel to Africa. In Africa hunters can continue their favorite sport and sell their kills to third parties. In turn the third parties process and sell the animals for mounted trophies, or butcher and package the meat for shipping to countries where people are willing to pay high prices for this scarce commodity. In order to keep up with the demand, increasing numbers of each hunted species are being killed. At the current rate of killing it is predicted that at least 90 percent of Africa's wild animal population will be wiped out by 2078.

Without Brad's knowledge, Doctor Monrovia recommended Brad to the United States Foreign Relations Bureau for a special project that would attempt to use a new pragmatic approach to again try to persuade one country at a time in Africa to stop hunting animals and eating meat. The project would require a two-year assignment in Zimbabwe, Africa. Each person chosen for this assignment by the Foreign Relations Bureau will have special talents and abilities, plus a proven record of kindness to animals.

Many sound theories support the belief that a large percentage of the deeply rooted traditions involving humans killing and eating dead animal flesh originated in prehistoric times on the continent of Africa.

It is understandable why a hunter would consider Africa a paradise. Countless descriptions of this large continent tell of the vast beauty and magnificent grandeur that surround the killing fields where a hunter can pursue many of the most beautiful and some of the most dangerous and most difficult-to-hunt animals on earth. Several books about hunting stress that experienced professional hunters often enjoy the hunt as much or more then the kill. They are experts at knowing every detail from A to Z needed in planning a successful safari. Many hunters admit they get satisfaction and some kind of high from the atmosphere surrounding them while they stalk and kill vast numbers of beautiful animals.

The part that is most disturbing and not understandable is if hunters get so much enjoyment out of the natural beauty of Africa and its marvelous animals, why do they feel the need to kill the animals? Did God create all the beautiful species of animals so that humans could brutally destroy them? Since when have cruelty and death been associated with beauty? If hunters have great respect and admiration for all the beauty and grandeur that Africa has to offer, why ruin it? Why not help the animals survive so they have a chance to live full lives?

When hunters desire to bring home memories of the trip, what is wrong with pictures or video movies that are much more enjoyable and should bring back fonder memories? Destroying a gorgeous animal so its head can be mounted on a family room wall does not exemplify kindness. A healthy, unharmed, living animal is certainly much more enjoyable to admire then a dead one.

Animals in Africa have enough problems trying to survive the attacks of other hungry animals. It adds another huge burden when they must also try to evade hunters carrying high-powered rifles who are constantly trying to destroy them. What could be more repulsive and a bigger unforgivable sin than to be surrounded by all the beauty Africa has to offer, and to express appreciation by stalking and killing animals?

The United States' beleaguered efforts have failed in Africa largely because they have not sent experienced persons qualified to understand Africa's multitude of diverse and ancient customs. The representatives from the United States until now accomplished very little, because they were completely naive regarding Africa's history. They tried to force-feed our anti-killing philosophy down the throats of people who have a very old culture and commerce that have relied heavily on meat consumption, meat trade, and hunting.

Obstinate African leaders, many whom are accomplished experienced professional hunters, were unimpressed with the audacious behavior of our politicians and health specialists that had previously tried to change their thinking.

On another beautiful Saturday morning Brad met with Dr. Monrovia at his seaside home. "Good morning, Doctor. I trust all is well with you, sir."

"Yes, Brad, all is well, and I am anxious to discuss an important issue with you. In my opinion the time has come for you to make much needed use of your knowledge about the benefits of protecting all animals. I have personally recommended that the United States government appoint you as an emissary to manage a group of animal protection experts in Zimbabwe, Africa.

- Arthur Poletti –

"The ultimate goal for all the members of your team during this two-year project will be the formidable task of convincing as many Africans as possible that cruelty toward and killing of animals, along with consumption of meat, is totally unnecessary. Government officials in the United States and Zimbabwe have been in close contact for many years as we have continually tried to convince them of the overall benefits of protecting all animal life, including the enormous health and agricultural benefits Americans have attained in a relatively short period of time.

"For fifty-seven years most animals in the United States have been fed much healthier vegetarian meat substitutes that have successfully replaced dead animal flesh; the animals are thriving. Throughout the United States large varieties of non-meat foods intended for wild animals are continuously distributed by agencies funded by the Federal government. This has been accomplished by continually filling thousands of different sizes of food troughs daily strategically located in animal reserves and sanctuaries throughout the country.

"Now we will be given the opportunity to apply the same principles on a continent that harbors millions of the most beautiful and many of the rarest animals on earth. Your group will attempt to convince and reform Zimbabwe's citizens and as many of their professional hunters as you can about the benefits of not killing.

"Our initial agreement with the Zimbabwean government is to work together for two years trying to prove the merits of our program. We hope that during the first two years using respectful diplomacy we will gain the interest of many other African countries that might be persuaded to begin a similar program. During and at the end of our initial two-year agreement, we will be openly available to assist in providing the same type of personnel to negotiate and initiate animal welfare programs separately with each interested country in Africa.

"In order to accomplish our main goal the project will begin with four objectives. The first objective is to convince the several hundred Zimbabwean citizens from every walk of life who have volunteered for the project that they can derive the same health

74

and prosperity we enjoy by not slaughtering animals or eating meat. These individuals have already agreed to begin eating only vegetarian foods and to continue doing so for at least two years. This is the first step in the process of eliminating meat from the food chain for humans and animals.

"During this period we will invite representatives from every country in African to visit and inspect our work sites. We hope they will then begin to try the same animal welfare procedures in their countries. Our intention again is to one day persuade all of the people of Africa to stop eating meat, to stop killing animals, and to eat only vegetarian foods.

"The second objective is to teach Zimbabwean cattle farmers how to utilize their land to grow and produce vegetarian foods for humans and animals. We need to prove to the farmers and their government that they can be far more successful using their land to produce healthier vegetarian foods than raising animals to be slaughtered.

"The third objective will be to use local food produce and large shipments of vegetarian foods from the United States to begin a major joint effort to feed Zimbabwe's entire animal population non-meat foods.

"I am certain that all animals, especially wild animals, when fed a variety of foods for several months that include meat substitutes will gradually become less aggressive, and their desire to stalk and kill other animals for food will be reduced." While our feeding programs will at first seem to be tedious, imperceptible, and inconsequential, in time animals will adapt to eating the large variety of healthy non-meat foods that are available and grown in many areas of the continent. Furthermore, by implementing the methods of spaying and neutering that became successful in the United States; the animal population in Zimbabwe will be humanely controlled and will continually decline to a manageable life supporting size.

"The fourth and most essential objective will be the addition and maintenance of several large animal reserves and sanctuaries that will be designed and developed to ultimately care for all of the reduced population of wild animals in Zimbabwe.

"The four objectives will begin simultaneously. Because of the natural language barriers that will exist we will need a show-and-tell, hands-on type of approach.

"Bradford, you must set the appropriate tone in our message to all of Africa's dignitaries by respectfully conforming to proper etiquette and protocol, which includes adhering to many different social amenities and religious customs.

"To enhance the effectiveness of our efforts you will need to select specialists from several professions, including veterinarian doctors, expert farmers, local food distributors, and language interpreters, along with representatives of the news media from around the world. Americans and Africans will work together. Also, because of the need to get close to dangerous animals, your team of experts will need the protection of dexterous Zimbabwean guides and professional hunters.

"We decided to recruit professional hunters from the ranks of African citizens who possess the acute knowledge, experience, and cumulative skills required for assisting and executing the close-up handling and feeding needed while being surrounded by wild, hungry animals. The hunters will be in full agreement not to attempt to kill any animal unless their lives or the lives of members of your team are in jeopardy. If this problem occurs, the hunters when possible will first attempt to immobilize any potentially threatening animal by using tranquilizers from dart guns.

"These procedures will ultimately create a far more civilized and healthy community for animals and people to live in.

"All of the members on your team would be wise to communicate frequently with as many of their professional colleagues as possible, explaining what we have accomplished in the United States since 2008, especially the major improvements in health, agriculture, and business, and the huge reductions in all crimes—amazing achievements resulting directly from the decision to stop killing animals and stop eating dead flesh.

"With this proof of the results Americans have achieved, Zimbabwe's leaders could be far more effective at convincing other citizens of the many benefits they would realize by not hunting and killing animals. An educated African professional hunter is well schooled in animal behavior, including their habits and tendencies when hunting for other animals. In addition, it is not unusual for African hunting guides to speak several languages, which will be very useful when trying to communicate and implement our program within every ethnic group in Zimbabwe.

"The most cumbersome physical obstacle to overcome will be confronting many dangerous and ferocious animals indigenous to Zimbabwe and neighboring countries that our members have never dealt with. Furthermore we have virtually no first-hand experience with many species of wild animals that roam throughout every country in Africa. Bradford, it will be unwise for you and your staff to wander around unprotected in the African bush trying to feed hungry animals veggie burgers! So you will be taught by experienced Africans some of the safest methods and optimal times of the day to feed the different species of animals, including reptiles and birds.

"Bradford, we are confronted with vastly different and more difficult challenges in Africa than we were confronted with and solved in the United States. However, we expect in time with perseverance and wisdom we will overcome the obstacles we will encounter. Our lifesaving procedures will be the catalyst leading eventually to laws that will create a solid infrastructure designed to protect all animal life from being killed for food, sport, or commerce, in every country of Africa.

"Do you have any questions?"

"Professor," Bradford replied, "I would be very excited to be a part of this long overdue effort; however, I recently became engaged to Alyssa and I would not be able to leave her behind."

"Bradford, please try to convince Alyssa to join you. Because of her education, knowledge, and love for animals, she could be hired to be your confidant and expert advisor. This effort will require a two-year commitment but will allow you and your staff vacation time and holiday leaves. Also, you and Alyssa will be required to make periodic trips with African officials to the

United States Foreign Bureau Office in Washington, D.C. The purpose will be to evaluate the progress being made and to hold round table meetings to listen to any suggestions that might enhance the chances for success."

Brad spent the next few hours having lunch with the professor and discussing the new adventure that he wanted to accept, but only if Alyssa would agree to join him.

During the drive home Brad thought about the animals in Africa. For as long as he could remember he had been disgusted by the cruelty to animals that has existed throughout the African continent for centuries. But he also realized that killing animals and eating meat in Africa had to stop, no matter how long it took or how impossible the task seemed.

The large scale of cruelty to animals that exists in Africa is not just isolated to the horrors inside of slaughterhouses or the vast numbers of animals killed by hunters. A huge problem is the ageless cruelty and death caused by wild animals killing wild animals for food.

Brad knew that many different species of well fed animals can be raised on a reserve or sanctuary together. When these animals are treated with kindness and compassion they are far less aggressive and rarely attempt to hunt and kill.

Years of experience monitoring animal behavior in the United States has proven that different species of animals raised together from birth while being fed non-meat foods can develop a natural affinity for each other. By instituting the same birth control methods of neutering or spaying and the same feeding procedures that have been so successful in the United States the population of animals and the total number of animals attempting to kill each other in Zimbabwe will be significantly reduced.

The overall goals can be accomplished by first beginning a continuous distribution of vast amounts of vegetarian foods to every area of Zimbabwe that animals reside, including the most remote areas. These foods will taste much like the foods fed to wild animals in the United States that proved to be an extremely successful substitute for dead flesh.

That evening Brad had a long conversation with his parents and Alyssa and was happy that Alyssa was in full agreement about working with him in Africa for the next two years.

Brad and Alyssa were married three months later on October 15 in Carmel, California, and then spent two weeks on their honeymoon in Maui, Hawaii. They were able to spend Thanksgiving and Christmas at home with their families before flying to Zimbabwe, Africa, to meet and join the new delegation of persons they would be working with for at least the next two years.

The animal rights successes in the United States could not be achieved in Africa without understanding and solving a number of problems that are unique to Africa. Doctor Monrovia had advised Brad that during the process of rapprochement and in order to prevail in persuading Africans to stop killing animals and eating dead flesh, he would first need to learn why the cruelty and killing has been so difficult to stop. Reasons which are directly related to Africans' ancient primordial habits.

Once the initial meetings, discussions, and speeches are completed, most of the members of the delegation will immediately begin the planned anticruelty programs, plus the procedures for replacing meat with vegetarian food for humans and animals in Zimbabwe. When the program is well under way, Brad, Alyssa, and other members of the group will begin a six- to eight-week trip traveling by helicopter to visit several other African countries. The sole purpose will be an attempt to get a better understanding of why all efforts in the past have failed to stop cruelty to animals in Africa.

On January 14, 2066, Brad and Alyssa arrived in Zimbabwe. On January 15, they were met at the United States embassy by their newly appointed staff of twenty-six people, along with local government dignitaries and news media representatives. Brad was introduced to a healthy, handsome; eighty-two-year-old man (who looked like he was fifty-two) named Michael Pacenti. A few minutes later Brad was absolutely shocked when he verified that Michael's father was the former professional hunter and meat eater, Mondo Pacenti.

Even more remarkable was the recommendation from the United States Foreign Ambassador that Michael Pacenti, because of his many accomplishments in the field of animal welfare and his eloquent oratory skills, should be the keynote speaker when the final presentation is made to Africans on January 23 at the Zimbabwe Coliseum.

Brad anxiously looked through his personnel files until he located Michael's resume and the government's report that revealed his many qualifications. Michael's professional career was mostly devoted to working for thirty-five years at the University of Illinois in Champaign, Illinois as a respected, successful, and popular veterinary doctor. For twenty-five years Michael was a member of the Physicians Committee for Responsible Medicine in Washington, D.C. In addition, he was often asked to speak at conventions and fundraising events generally sponsored by animal activist groups. In November of 2006, when Michael was twenty-four years old, he accepted a position as a member of a special committee appointed by the Congress of the United States to help formulate the new Animal Welfare Act that was officially instituted in 2008.

Michael got married in 2007 and has been married to the same woman for fifty-eight years. Together they raised three children: two daughters and a son. Young Michael Pacenti's formal education was filled with curriculum related to many aspects of animal life. During his high school years Michael worked part time for several different animal rescue and welfare organizations. He graduated from the University of Illinois and obtained a doctorate degree in Animal Sciences and Medicines at the Boston University School of Medicine.

Brad could not wait to speak to Michael privately to ask him about his childhood. When he got a chance he said, "Michael, please spend a few minutes with me and tell me how you became so involved with animal welfare."

"Sir, my father, Mondo Pacenti, was mostly responsible for teaching me about the virtues of kindness and the importance of protecting and caring for all animal life. He would be proud to know that I have tried to follow in his footsteps and will promote many of his ideas during this historic effort on behalf of all animal life."

While Bradford listened to Michael speak, tears began to appear in his eyes. He had difficulty controlling his emotions as he thought about Mondo Pacenti and what a wonderful influence he had been to his son.

"Michael, the United States Foreign Ambassador has recommended that you deliver the keynote speech on January 23. After reviewing the government report disclosing your many achievements and your lifetime devoted to animal welfare, I agree that you are the right choice. I only wish your father could be here to witness your special presentation." They shook hands and parted.

The remainder of the afternoon was filled with many activities. Most of Brad's new team had thought-provoking conversations, exchanging ideas and plans while confirming each individual's responsibilities, making ready to embark on their joint adventure.

Brad had prepared a speech that he was about to present just as his guests were finishing a lavish, sumptuous, vegetarian dinner. He utilized information gathered from reading several books about Africa's history including pertinent details obtained from several African members of his staff. Brad intended to give everyone an overview of how the anti-cruelty to animals programs would begin. He planned to identify some of the obstacles to overcome, and the overall goals that needed to be achieved, first in Zimbabwe and hopefully in a few short years throughout all of Africa.

"Good evening ladies and gentlemen," he began. "On behalf of all the wonderful animals that live in Africa, we are all excited and eager to begin our work. Let me first summarize some of the important details that we have learned about Africa and the obstacles we will need to overcome to be successful at promoting a lasting program of anticruelty throughout the continent. Many of the proven benefits that we have realized in the United States by not killing animals and not eating meat can potentially be realized by large numbers of people in every country of Africa.

"The population of Africa is about 860 million people, of which about two thirds live in rural areas; the remainder lives in towns and cities. The population has increased very rapidly because of a high birthrate, despite an average life expectancy of only 53 years, compared with about 112 years for Americans.

"In the poorer countries of the continent like Zambia, the life expectancy is 37 years. In the more developed nations of Africa people live longer. For example, in Libya life expectancy is about 75 years and in Tunisia 69 years. Africa has one of the highest death rates in the world. People in many areas of the continent suffer from malnutrition and for many years famines have killed millions.

"Poor sanitation and inadequate medical services have contributed to widespread disease. Some of the most serious diseases include aids, malaria, and bovine spongiform encephalopathy, commonly known as mad cow disease, tuberculosis, yellow fever, and sleeping sickness.

"Nearly two million Asians live in southern and eastern Africa. Most are descendents of people who came to Africa from India during the 1800s. More then eight hundred languages are spoken in Africa, which can make communication among Africans very difficult.

"A large number of educated Africans speak English, French, and Portuguese, plus their local language. There are hundreds of local religions in Africa with each ethnic group having its own set of beliefs. It is important to note that all African religions recognize the existence of a supreme God. About 155 million Africans are Muslims and their religion is Islam. Nearly 135 million Africans are Christians, mostly Roman Catholics and Protestants.

"Africa has great mineral wealth, including huge deposits of copper, diamonds, gold, and petroleum. Many African rivers and waterfalls could be used to produce hydroelectric power. Agriculture is the leading economic activity in Africa, but most farmers use outdated tools and methods to farm thin, poor soil. Africa also has the least developed economy of any continent except Antarctica. The development of manufacturing has been handicapped by a lack of money to build factories, a shortage of skilled workers, and competition from industries on other continents. Many African countries depend on only one or two farm or mineral products for more than half their export earnings.

"Africa's abundance of valuable forests, grasslands, and natural plant life has been significantly reduced. Farmers have cleared forests for cropland and hunters have repeatedly burned grasslands to drive out game animals. The overgrazing by livestock has turned formerly productive land into deserts. The majority of African nations rely heavily on aid from countries outside the continent.

"Africa's wild animals are world famous. They include thousands of species of reptiles, fish, birds, and insects.

"Several African countries have taken steps to save their rich wildlife heritage. Fortunately, the killing of certain animals is prohibited in many areas. Also, a number of African countries have established game reserves and national parks.

"Hunting is forbidden in these areas, and modern methods of wildlife conservation are practiced to protect the animals. Many hunters go on carefully regulated safaris, which are hunting expeditions. Other people go on photographic safaris to gain memories of live animals in their natural environments. However, poaching (illegal hunting) continues to be a serious problem.

"Many rural Africans have opposed wildlife conservation efforts, especially in areas where wild animals compete with farmers and herders for scarce land. Wild animals have been known to destroy an entire crop or threaten the lives of villagers and their farm animals. Animal meat is important to the welfare of some Africans, and people accused of illegal hunting may actually be struggling to feed their families.

"We intend to plant the seeds of knowledge, awareness, and hope to improve the lives of all animals in Africa. Initially, however, we will focus more time on feeding a few selected species in order to measure results more quickly.

"To begin to reduce the number of attempts ravenous animals make to kill each other for food, we will begin feeding large amounts of vegetarian foods to cheetahs, hyenas, jackals, leopards, and lions that generally prey on antelopes, buffaloes, giraffes, zebras, and baboons. We will also devote considerable time to feeding the chimpanzees and monkeys that dwell in many of the forests, as well as crocodiles and hippopotamuses that live in tropical rivers and swamps.

"Each day caravans of trucks will transport substantial quantities of vegetarian foods to every area of Zimbabwe. We will continually distribute foods that taste much like the foods fed to wild animals in the United States that have proven to be an extremely successful substitute for dead flesh. Veterinarians, guides, and hunters will work together to accomplish the task of tranquilizing large numbers of wild animals in order to perform the birth control measures of spaying and neutering.

"Preparations are currently underway in Zimbabwe to begin a systematic process of converting thousands of acres of land currently used for cattle farms and cattle ranches into large animal reserves and sanctuaries. The augmentation of our plan will be to continually acclimatize wild animals into this new safer environment.

"By the end of our two year project we hope to set a positive example by providing at least 50% of the wild animals in Zimbabwe a safe haven. The expansion of large reserves and sanctuaries will proceed until all wild animals in Zimbabwe are accounted for and an open invisible wall of protection surrounds them.

"This is just a brief synopsis of how we will attempt to overcome obstacles, achieve our goals, and have a better understanding of the people we are dealing with. We will use discretion each step of the way as we develop solid evidence that will confirm the many benefits all Africans can share when they nourish and protect their beautiful animals and stop eating meat.

"By using most farmland for produce rather than cattle, and changing eating habits to vegetarian foods, the overall health of all Africans and the welfare of all animal life will have the potential to improve immensely.

"Just as we did in the United States, we must also convince as many people as possible of the spiritual benefits that can be felt from supporting the right of every animal to have a full and safe life. May the seeds of kindness be nurtured in every African.

"Thank you for listening to me. I hope you enjoy the remainder of the evening."

Chapter Ten

There Are No Slaughterhouses in Heaven

Michael Pacenti's official presentation was planned for 9 a.m. on Sunday, January 23rd, at the Zimbabwe coliseum. Between twenty-five and thirty thousand people including dignitaries, citizens, and news media representatives from every country in Africa were expected to attend the eight-hour program. The program had been carefully planned by United States officials, with considerable help and input from Africans.

Brad took Alyssa's advice and provided Michael Pacenti with copies of his final examination presentation given at the University of California. Together Brad and Michael would select the parts that seemed most appropriate and meaningful for the mostly African audience. Michael had carefully prepared material for his own speech, but after reviewing the information from Brad's college presentation he agreed to recite parts of several sections.

For three eight-hour days, Brad and Michael met and exchanged ideas with many Africans, with the help of American and African interpreters. All pertinent information was considered, including a final review to recapitulate the materials Brad used for his college presentation. The four language interpreters would need considerable time to translate Michael's words effectively for the many different Africans speaking and understanding numerous dialects. So it was decided that Michael make his keynote speech as short and as informative as possible, preferably not longer then eight hours.

Michael sought out additional suggestions and recommendations from several American and African staff members regarding ways to effectively impress African citizens and gain their endorsement of the program.

The most difficult obstacle for Michael would be to present the case for the importance of protecting animals without insulting or offending the diverse audience, which would include representatives from every country on the African continent. Even though Michael would be eager to share his knowledge, he would need to be diplomatic. A slow process would be needed to allow all participants to better understand and overcome the barriers of language, cultural habits, and religious faiths. Then the goal of persuading impervious Africans to stop eating meat and stop killing animals could be gradually achieved.

During the same period of time, Brad's team would attempt to prove that wild animals could be fed many foods other then meat that are far better for their health. This would be accomplished by providing vegetarian foods on a large-scale basis to wild and domestic animals in and out of captivity. In the United States since September 1, 2008, with few exceptions, wild and domesticated animals have been fed only non-meat foods. These animals are much healthier, live longer, and have proven that over time they and their offspring continually exhibit, on a declining scale, far less of the aggressive instincts to attack and eat other animals.

At 8 a.m. on January 23, 2066, preliminary ceremonies by African and American dignitaries marked the beginning of what Brad hoped would in time lead to a monumental achievement in all of Africa.

The United States' foreign ambassador and then the amiable governor of Zimbabwe made a few opening announcements while a large number of people continued to enter the coliseum. Then at 8:50 a.m., as the ambassador introduced Michael Pacenti to the crowd, he was warmly greeted with loud applause.

"Good morning, ladies and gentlemen, and thank you for your greetings," began Michael. Let me also thank you, mister foreign ambassador, all members of the government, local dignitaries, and citizens of Zimbabwe for the opportunity you have given us.

"It seems that God and nature worked in conjunction for centuries to create a paradise in which to provide and bestow the plentiful natural resources, lavish splendors, and quintessence that exists throughout Africa, including an abundance of many of the most beautiful species of animals in the world.

"Unfortunately in Africa, centuries of unnecessary crimes committed against animals for food, sport, and cruel experimentation seems to have permanently preserved and fueled the precarious never-ending tragic curse that throughout recorded history has continuously caused epidemics of old and new diseases, plagues, and never-ending violent crimes. The origin, development, and presence of most diseases and violent crimes in Africa can be traced back to the transmission to humans of terrified and diseased cells from the dead flesh of brutally killed animals.

"Many seasoned veterans of hunting seem to feel as strongly about their right and need to kill animals as animal rights activists feel about protecting animals. The following is a quote made by Jose Ortega Gasset one of the more famous supporters of hunting.

Hunting is an escape that is necessary for man as a form of preservation of his sanity. It is a pursuit that man alone follows as an avocation, as recreation. It is one of the most highly individualistic activities of men. It is man alone against the wild animals, in a unique situation not repeated elsewhere in all of nature. It is an activity for which there is no substitute. There is no possible substitution through simulation. One either hunts, or one does not hunt. It permits no middle ground.

"Please remember the above statement. It is incomprehensible, to put it mildly. There must be better ways to preserve one's own sanity besides hunting! The hunters and meat eater's habit of overlooking the cruelty and brutal killing of animal life must once and for all come to an end. Otherwise the alliance between animals and humans will continue declining to a complete and final destruction.

"Unbelievably, meat eaters in Africa seem to disregard all the proven facts about the health hazards directly related to meat consumption. With all the cruelty, death, and disease that have resulted from killing animals and eating their flesh, animal rights organizations, vegans, and vegetarians find it hard to believe that laws have not been instituted in every country in Africa to stop the carnage immediately.

"Religious beliefs older than Christianity, known as Hinduism and Jainism, clearly insist that animals should never be treated cruelly. Hindus teach vegetarianism as a way to live with a minimum of hurt to other beings. They believe that when humans consume meat, fish, or fowl, they participate indirectly in acts of cruelty and violence against the animal kingdom. The meat eater's desire for meat drives another to kill and provide that meat. The act of the butcher begins with the desire of the consumer. Meat eating contributes to a mentality of violence, and from the chemically complex meat one absorbs the slaughtered creature's fear, pain, and terror.

"There are different levels of compassion expressed by humans towards animals. Especially among those who profess to love animals. There are also major differences of opinion between meat eaters and vegans. We all say we love our pets, but if you are a meat eater you are subconsciously condoning the brutal slaughter of animals daily that is needed to feed the mouths of the world's remaining population of dead flesh eaters. Eating meat does not express the purest form of love for the animal world.

"Since humans, not God, were responsible for writing all the words for every religious faith, they can be blamed for some of the disingenuous, self-serving, thoughtless connotations written in the Bible that could not possibly have been authorized or ordained by God. Words that cleverly dismissed the immense value, importance, and absolute necessity of protecting every animal's life.

"For centuries, with a few important exceptions, most religions conveniently ignored the importance of protecting all animal life. The Bible was filled with ambiguous scriptures written by men for the benefit of people, not animals. Nevertheless, it is impossible to believe that any God worthy of worshipping has ever, or would ever, give authorization to humans to destroy animals and eat their flesh.

"There can be no bigger sin than the affectation and the manipulation of scriptures in the Bible to justify and satisfied the inherited and ageless human cravings to kill animals and eat their flesh.

"Take heed, and beware, a genuine God can not be manipulated, and will not be a partner blind to false religious interpretations. Such as verses that cleverly appeared in the Bible over 2000 years ago for the sole purpose of making it seem as though God authorized man to destroy animals and eat their flesh.

"Do you think that any God worthy of your worship would arbitrarily authorize the worldwide mass destruction of creature's lives so that humans can eat their flesh?

"Do you think there are slaughterhouses in heaven?

"Do you think that supporting cruelty and killing animals for your consumption will be rewarded with kindness, love, and nirvana in your next life? How many meat eaters would support their religious beliefs or attend church if they were told that cruelty to animals and eating meat is an unforgivable sin?

"The demand for religious clarity regarding animals persuaded amenable leaders representing every faith throughout the world to deliberate and resolve obvious improprieties in the Bible. After considerable evaluation the prudent decision was finally made to amend and or delete verses in the Holy Bible that insinuate God authorized or seemed to authorize any form of cruelty to animals.

"The final determination for the long over due religious accord was based on the absolute   bona-fide belief that almighty God would never condone, support, permit, or promote cruelty, violence or premature death to animals. Furthermore, cruelty in any form is the complete *antithesis* of what God represents. As you all know the amended version of the Holy Bible was released throughout the world in December, 2012."

"We know that all humans are born and all will die. What we are not certain of is what happens to a human's soul after death.

"Theologically speaking it seems reasonable to believe that a person that devotes their life to supporting and promoting cruelty to any of God's living creatures will not realize the same after death experience as a person that devotes their life to supporting and promoting kindness to all living creatures."

"There is an ancient religious theory that insists that humans who eat the flesh of animals will be punished for their cruelty. Many will suffer physical and mental pain periodically throughout their lifetime from any one of a variety of illnesses and diseases caused by consuming dead animal flesh. Sounds crazy to you? Don't be so sure this could not happen! Why take the chance?

"A nation that is capable of limitless sacrifice is capable of rising to limitless heights. The purer the sacrifice the quicker the progress."

Mahatma Gandhi

"Ask yourself these questions and carefully consider your answers. If you personally had to kill a cow or pig to eat their dead flesh, would you do it, especially when there are plenty of other choices of food that are much healthier for you?

"How would you feel if you saw your own pets brutally slaughtered and eaten? Every time you look at or eat a piece of meat, remember that animal wanted to live just as much as your pets want to live.

"Hunters and meat eaters might want to reconsider whether killing animals or eating their dead bodies really adds value, quality, or good health to their lives. Hunters who have pets at home should think about why they are willing to love, protect, and care for their own pets but do not express similar feelings when they stalk and kill wild animals.

"Killing animals and eating their dead flesh should have stopped a long time ago. We can not change the past; however, we certainly have the ability to change the future. Each one of you who is a meat eater or hunter needs to clearly realize the difference between cruelty and kindness.

"Imagine what God is thinking while he stands at the doorstep of every slaughterhouse in Africa to witness the procedures of cruelty and death administered to thousands of animals.

"Imagine what God is thinking while he stands at the doorstep of every laboratory in Africa to witness the brutal torture and destruction of animals during experimentations.

"Imagine what God is thinking while he watches every hunter in Africa that stalks and cruelly ends the lives of precious animals that God put on earth to be loved and protected. Sacred lives that deserve the God given right to be unharmed and to live in peaceful harmony with the universe.

"These unforgivable cardinal sins are the result of unnecessary crimes committed to animals caused by complete unawareness of the precious value and absolute sanctity of every creature's life.

"The destruction of animals fuels and promotes prosperity for the devil and his biggest allies, cruelty, violence and premature death.

"Cruelty is demonstrated when you participate in any part of the vicious cycle of killing and consuming animal flesh.

"Kindness is demonstrated when you do not participate in any part of the vicious cycle of killing and consuming animal flesh.

"Parents throughout Africa need to understand and be convinced that all animals deserve the right to live a full life filled with affection, love, and protection much like they express to their own children. Parents need to set examples every day by their own actions and continually explain to their children the importance of being kind and compassionate to all living creatures.

"On a much brighter note, I have wonderful news for you. In order to begin protecting all of the animals of Africa, progressive political representatives from the government of Zimbabwe considered and are now willing to try new methods to protect and conserve your precious animal life.

"Fifty-seven years ago Americans began a similar program to protect animals. I was fortunate to be one of the legislative committee members who helped formulate several important laws that the United States Congress incorporated into the Animal Welfare Act of 2008. The revolutionary new laws were designed primarily to forbid humans to eat dead animal flesh and to protect animals from being brutally killed or treated cruelly. We knew that meat could be replaced by much healthier foods that would be far more beneficial to our citizens.

"The success we have achieved for the benefit of animals and people has established a remarkable precedent that is mind boggling.

"Today in America we have proven that by not raising cattle to be slaughtered, we are far more prosperous, we're healthier, and we live longer. We must impress you with the enormous magnitude of benefits we realize throughout our society today as a result of being kind to animals.

"In order to make you aware of the many benefits Africans would realize by not killing animals for food or sport, I will read to you applicable excerpts from different parts of a presentation made by my colleague, Bradford Knox, just a few months ago.

"The title of the presentation he made to his classmates at the University of California is How Kindness To Animals Has Changed The World."

Michael's speech lasted nearly nine hours including a thirty minute break for lunch and a few brief pauses. He thanked the large audience for listening and began the last stages of the program by introducing and reciting a famous verse.

"I believe that animals have their own religion, a religion not motivated by greed, possessions, or a promise to go to heaven.

Even though animals cannot read, write, or speak our languages, they have a way of bonding with humans by expressing and receiving the purest form of love and devotion. In part their religion was summarized beautifully by Walt Whitman in the following verse.

I think I could turn and live with animals.
They are so placid and self-contained.
I stand and look at them long and long.
They do not sweat and whine about their condition.
They do not lie awake in the dark and weep for their sins.
They do not make me sick discussing their duty to God.
Not one is dissatisfied; not one is demented with the mania of
owning things.
Not one kneels to another, nor to his kind that lived thousands of
years ago.
Not one is respectable or unhappy over the whole earth.

Michael smiled at the audience for several seconds and then said.

"It has been said that what one can receive from another is a thought, a question, but the exploration has to be one's own. Unless your reasoning ability and conscious thought discover the truth, it is not the truth for you; it is only a description of the truth.

"For the sake of your families welfare, especially the prospects of a better life for your children, please consider the many benefits of protecting every animals life.

"I would like to ask each person in the audience and every person in every country of Africa to reach into the hidden caverns of your soul to seek truth and guidance. Only there will you discover how you really feel about the value and importance of protecting every creature's life.

"In memory of my father, Mondo Pacenti, I will begin the last segments of this program by reciting one of his favorite

Hindu verses written by Tirumantira, and than I will recite a poem that I have always admired written by Rumi.

"Many are the lovely flowers of worship offered to the Guru, but none lovelier than non-killing. Respect for life is the highest worship, the bright lamp, the sweet garland, and unwavering devotion.

"What do you really possess, and what have you gained? What pearls have you brought up from the depths of the sea? On the day of death, bodily senses will vanish. Do you have the spiritual light to accompany your heart? When dust fills these eyes in the grave, will your grave shine bright?"

Michael paused, looked at the audience for a few moments, and then continued.

"My father believed that when a person has psychologically achieved a desire from their soul to be kind to all living creatures in every way then they have arrived at the place they should be. He emphasized that a person should not think it is a special achievement when they are kind to animals, but rather realize they are doing what is appropriate and expected. My father often recited the following words of wisdom to me, which I think of often.

"Let us have the sense of justice to check up from time to time the quality and the nature of our own beliefs. In the light of new data gained, in the presence of new ideas accepted, the old belief may have to be changed in its form or content. At such moments let us have the courage to make the necessary changes to remodel the existing belief.

"Let us always have the courage to check within ourselves to repair, to refine our convictions, our beliefs, and our way-of -life.

Michael paused for several seconds then continued with his own thoughts.

"Most humans hope or expect that their lives will continue after death, and pray they will end up in a better place. Others think that when humans die they remain in a perpetual state of oblivion, dead forever in a deep dark hole.

"One of the most essential prerequisites for an eternal life of happiness may be directly related to whether or not you have been cruel or kind to all living creatures, human and animal.

"Certainly if there is a heaven, you can be sure that animals are not tortured, killed, and eaten there. Therefore, since there is no meat in heaven, now might be a good time to change your eating habits.

"Cruelty does not exist in heaven, but being cruel may be the surest method for a person to obtain a box seat in hell. This is a personal choice we all make in our lives.

"Will your choice be to continue supporting cruelty and death, or will each one of you seriously consider seeking your own personal redemption in the eyes of God?

"You can begin to accomplish this goal by being an important and intricate part of a worldwide effort attempting to provide the prospect of a full and safe life for all animals.

Michael, a charismatic speaker, paused for several moments to glance at the enthralled attentive audience, and then he continued.

"May some of the dormant hidden seeds of kindness in your soul be rekindled and then blossom in your conscious mind. May you then be inspired to join our righteous campaign to permanently protect the sanctity of life for all creatures on the face of the earth.

"Clearly, when this crusade is over your heart will tell you which society you would prefer to live in.

"My father Mondo Pacenti believed, and convinced me to believe, that when you attempt to rescue or protect any of Gods creatures from the ravages of cruelty, you will in turn, rescue a part of your own soul.

"May your sincere affections and sympathy for animal's lives generate love, compelling you to seek an identity with this cause.

"I believe God sees each one of us for what we really are, not necessarily what we profess to be. He knows whether we are genuine or a fraud.

"May each person in the audience and every person living in every country in Africa seriously consider how your own rendezvous with destiny may unfold?

"May God have mercy on your soul?"

The audience was completely silent as Michael began to walk away from the podium. Only the echoing sounds that resonated from different species of chattering animals in the jungle nearby could be heard.

Bradford Knox was absolutely amazed at the quality and persuasive force of Michael's presentation. Even more amazing was how Michael's brilliant father, the former professional hunter and meat eater named Mondo Pacenti had nurtured the seeds of kindness in young Michael's mind. Seeds that blossomed into a life of excellent health, peace, non-violence, and spiritual prosperity for Michael and his family.

Bradford vividly remembered the society that Mondo was raised in, surrounded by reprehensible cruelty, violence, and death to animals and people for most of his life. What Brad did not know was that long ago Mondo had decided to put down his guns and became a spokesman for the value of protecting and preserving all animal life.

Mondo was able to find his own spiritual truth through meaningful inquiry. This was accomplished by first freeing and detaching himself from all former belief, prejudices, conclusions and conditioning. Only then was Mondo, the former expert hunter and meat eater able to develop real wisdom from within and make a truly meaningful and heart felt decision regarding the precious value of all animal life.

Bradford now truly believed that Mondo Pacenti was a better man than he, accomplishing an amazing feat against overwhelming odds. When a person can go against the status quo with unyielding determination to set an example of the power of kindness for the benefit of his family, his friends, and especially animals, then that person has reached the pinnacle of success. Unequivocal proof that nonviolence combined with kindness and compassion is the greatest religion!

Mahatma Gandhi said it best:

Nonviolence is the greatest force at the disposal of mankind. It is mightier than the mightiest weapon of destruction devised by the ingenuity of men.

The End

Epilogue

A small percentage of the total animal population is fortunate to be selected to be our companions. These domesticated creatures satisfy our needs as we exchange and express the purest feelings of kindness, devotion, trust, and love. Unfortunately, for most of the billions of unlucky animals remaining, their quality of life goes from bad to horrendous. They are not held and comforted. They are not given names. Their living conditions could not be worse. Each year billions suffer from the pain of continuous never ending cruelty followed by excruciating death. They end their abbreviated lives in slaughterhouses so that humans can have the needless unhealthy luxury of eating their dead flesh.

One of the most bizarre phenomena is that there are millions of people who truly love and protect their pets while making a sincerely kind and considerate effort to provide the best possible life for them. However, most of the same people love eating meat and many are hunters who think nothing of killing wild animals. This is a cruel double standard.

Years of news stories around the globe revealing catastrophic disasters related to meat consumption and threats of major epidemics that may be caused by diseases like Mad Cow, E.coli, and the H5N1 virus or bird flu, has convinced millions of people that consuming any of God's creatures is unhealthy and, in some cases, life threatening. It's become increasingly obvious that eating animals promotes and supports the worst kind of cruelty, and is completely unnecessary.

Current consumer awareness has created a dilemma for the meat industry. Conservatively it is estimated that as many as 6 to 8 percent of United States citizens are currently vegetarians. This figure could easily stretch to 9 to 10 percent by the end of 2006. There are approximately 300 million people in the United States today. This means that there may be at least 27 to 30 million vegetarians in the country by the year 2007 and the actual figure may end up being much higher.

In addition, many meat eaters are now encountering more and more vegetarian options and meat alternatives at their local supermarkets. It is likely that a large number of those who are on the fence could be convinced to make the healthier and morally correct change soon.

If all humans can survive perfectly well and consume much healthier food without the need to kill animals, why do laws throughout the world support hunting and why do most people support cruelty toward and slaughter of animals, and the worthless destructive habit of eating meat? Many famous business leaders and celebrities, as well as kings, queens, emperors, empresses, and presidents from most countries in the world throughout history have hunted and killed animals. They have approved, supported, and passed on the torch of death to each generation in favor of eating animal flesh.

These massive atrocities are still permitted and are going on every second of the day around the world to keep filling the tummies of billions of dead flesh eaters. Bad habits, even when pathetically cruel and totally unnecessary, are hard to change. Humans should not be proud of being known as the most prolific and dangerous predators on earth.

Nevertheless, you can choose to change your habits. Consider the following simple acts of kindness to live by that you may want to begin today!

Do not kill animals or eat their dead flesh.

Do not support or participate in any act of cruelty to any living creature. Remember, animals do not need to die so that you can eat.

Finally, consider some words of wisdom from one of the oldest religions on earth:

KARMA is the law of action and reaction at work in the moral universe.

Every thought, word, and action produces an effect that rebounds on the person, or the culture that generated it, often referred to as KARMIC consequences.

Commentary On Vegetarianism

by Swami Chinmayananda

Question: Why is vegetarian food considered better in India?

Answer: Eat we must. What we like to eat depends upon one's taste. There are only four things available – stones, plants, animals, and humans. Unfortunately we cannot eat stones because our system is not geared to digest and assimilate them directly. And even though we sometimes destroy human beings with our cruelty, our progressive culture does not allow eating them. That leaves us the vegetable and animal kingdom to choose from. No doubt, since prehistoric times, animals have been eaten, but we find that the very first progenitor of humanity, Adam himself, was eating only vegetables. It is only his second son who started this easy method of obtaining food because agriculture seemed to be too difficult for him, as it required a continuous process of putting forward effort in order to produce. Whereas sitting behind a stone, waiting for innocent animals to come along, and destroying and eating them seemed to be the easier way!

Question: How did the idea of vegetarianism develop in India?

Answer: We learned that vegetables can stay fresh up to forty - eight hours, but meat deteriorates and becomes harmful very quickly. Furthermore, within the human body, during the process of digestion, food remains in the digestive system for about forty-eight hours.

Fruit and vegetables digest much faster than meat. Whatever stays longer in the intestines starts to decay with the heat of the body system, which creates a lot of toxins.

Let me explain this idea of toxicity a little more. You must have noticed that generally man eats other animals. It is very difficult for man to digest and assimilate carnivorous animals.

This suggests that they must be highly toxic to his system. It also suggests that a certain amount of toxicity is present in the first round of eaten animals, because twice removed the meat of carnivorous animals becomes impossible to eat!

Question: In what way does vegetarian food help a person's mind? Did people discover that it affects the mental temperament?

Answer: The food that we take in and the thoughts and actions that spring forth from us have a distinct relationship. In the computer world, there is a well known saying, garbage in, garbage out. This seems to be true of our bodies as well. If you put toxic food – garbage – into your system, in the long run the texture of your thoughts and actions have a tendency to become extremely selfish, less concerned for others, and lusty, and therefore potentially dangerous to the social order.

Thus we can see that toxins in the system bring about a lot of mental disturbances. The same principle applies to drinking alcohol. Since our culture is essentially geared for the life of meditation, the mind that is constantly agitated and wandering finds it difficult to plunge into meditation. To such an individual, the toxin is an obstacle in reaching his goal. Probably this must have been the reason why; the rishis in the jungles ate only fruits, roots, leaves, and drank water. Those who eat non-vegetarian food may be very uncontrolled because of toxins in their food. Watch a vegetarian and a non-vegetarian animal. All herbaceous animals are available for eating; whereas the non-vegetarian or carnivorous animals are never eaten, even by hard core non-vegetarians.

Why is this?

Because carnivorous animals have got so much toxicity in them that it means almost death to eat them.

Printed in the United States
52938LVS00008B/57

9 781846 852312